"Why don't you have a woman?" she asked, still breathing hard.

"I have one tonight."

"Oh, you are more than any other man could ever be."

What a lovely female. God made some women to be loved, and she fit that role perfectly. No restraint, no superstitions, no guilt—she gave her all to the last moment and beyond.

"What bothers me about you—"

"No, you don't know anything about me. I am a wanted man, and so I must change my job, identity, and location, without notice, to prevent my enemies from capturing me."

"I know places in western Montana and Idaho where no one could find us. Maybe they could find a tribe, but never find two lovers. Do you believe me?"

"That place must be heaven." He used his index finger to raise her chin and then softly kissed her lips. No place was safe. Wilderness or not, it wouldn't be trackless for men who were anxious to find him. He was better on the move than pinned down. Someday, some drunk would say, "Oh, I saw him in Billings on Sunday," and they'd rush to sniff out any trail.

"My dear, you are the loveliest woman in bed I could ever imagine." He kissed her and then started to get up.

"No, sleep with me."

"We won't sleep."

"Who cares? You have warmed my heart."

JAKE LOGAN

SLOCUM AND THE CHEYENNE PRINCESS

JOVE BOOKS, NEW YORK

THE BERKLEY PUBLISHING GROUP
Published by the Penguin Group
Penguin Group (USA) LLC
375 Hudson Street, New York, New York 10014

USA • Canada • UK • Ireland • Australia • New Zealand • India • South Africa • China

penguin.com

A Penguin Random House Company

SLOCUM AND THE CHEYENNE PRINCESS

A Jove Book / published by arrangement with the author

For information, address: The Berkley Publishing Group,
a division of Penguin Group (USA) LLC,
375 Hudson Street, New York, New York 10014.

ISBN: 978-0-515-15489-4

PUBLISHING HISTORY
Jove mass-market edition / August 2014

PRINTED IN THE UNITED STATES OF AMERICA

10 9 8 7 6 5 4 3 2 1

Cover illustration by Sergio Giovine.

1

War-painted bucks concealed behind juniper, elder brush, and boulders on the hillside fired their rifles, and puffs of gun smoke drifted upward. Every once in a while, one of their lead bullets struck a taut canvas wagon cover with a loud pop. The wagon train men were behind the circled thirty freight wagons, either on their bellies or swabbing out their rifle bores with brushes on long rods. The midday heat made Slocum remove his felt hat and wipe out the hatband sweat with his kerchief. Hell of a damn deal. At least his livestock was in the corral of circled rigs, and most were alive and none seriously wounded so far.

One of the freighters took a shot, and at the loud explosion, Slocum swore out loud. "Damnit, if you can't hit one of them red devils, save your ammo. We're going to need those bullets, and they won't come back for us to use them."

"Ira got him dead on with his Sharps fifty-caliber," someone yelled from the north side.

"I'm not complaining about that. I mean just dumb shooting."

"Aye, sir."

"How long are they going to stay out there?" The question came from someone resting on his belly underneath a wagon bed, with just his dusty run-over boots showing. He, no doubt, was watching for any movement from the attackers.

"Hell, if I knew that, I'd have joined Custer and saved his ass at the Little Big Horn."

"Hell, that sumbitch probably knocked up your daughter."

"I don't have any."

"How do you know? You may have had several. You've sowed enough seed out here."

Amused, Slocum shook his head. "Keep your eyes on them, men."

"Slocum, are these Arapahos?"

"That, and Cheyenne."

"Who's their chief?"

"If I knew that, I'd call him out for a parley."

"Yeah, and he'd probably eat you for supper."

"Watch for them, boys. When they move on us, it will be quick."

If the Indians didn't initiate another raid by sundown, he aimed to slip outside to spy on them and see what he could find out about his enemy. Indians were bad about having big war parties to celebrate before they struck the next day. If they had any firewater, they'd get drunk as hell, too. If they did, and he had a chance to kill them, several would never wake up to fight.

In another day, the wagon train water supply would be used up out of the barrels strapped on the sides of each freight wagon. That meant Slocum needed to end this siege within the next twenty-four hours. Chances of an army patrol coming by to rescue them were slim to none. He hadn't expected such an active war party, but the Bozeman Trail hadn't ever been a healthy road to Montana, not even a year after Custer's demise.

His train was loaded with farm equipment. He'd left out of Omaha late, hoping to reach the Billings country with the freight before fall. A riverboat on the Missouri River in early spring might have been a better choice to ship it, but they could haul settlers for more money than what the freight would pay for space.

So he told Charlie Hackett he'd do his best to get the implement freight up there before the snowflakes flew. The trip so far had been a hard, hot, dusty job, but they'd had hardly any breakdowns or setbacks while they crawled like ants westward and then northward. In fact, they were way ahead of what Slocum called his mental schedule when this band of two dozen or so warriors picked them out as a prime prize. If they knew the wagons were only carrying pitchforks and mowing machines, they'd never have stopped them. All the Indians he'd ever known weren't interested in any such instruments of labor.

Before sundown, he talked to Indian Joe, a tough Sac-Fox Indian he'd hired in Omaha. There was also Buster Johnson, who he'd added in Fort Laramie, and an ex-army teamster who called himself Whethers. The four parleyed by themselves over some fresh coffee, squatting in the Wyoming dust to make plans for the night.

"If they have a powwow tonight and get drunk, we should be able to cut enough throats to make them think about leaving or not charging us again. Either way, we damn sure need to get on up to that Tongue River."

Buster spit tobacco juice aside. "We sure do need to do that."

"I'm going to use a buffalo hide to conceal myself," Slocum said. "Each man should have two revolvers, but don't use them unless you can't use a knife. If you get in trouble, we'll try to come to your aid, but one gunshot will bring the camp down on whoever fires it."

"What if we can stampede their horses?" Joe asked.

"That would damn sure work," Slocum agreed. The loss of their horses would be a big blow to their plans.

"They usually have boys wrangling them. They aren't hard to sneak up on."

Slocum agreed. These three men knew their business. "Around three o'clock on the Big Dipper we all should be back here in camp. Each of us will slip out in different directions, so they don't notice. You men know how to fight Injuns. Do it."

The three men nodded. They rose, drank the last of their coffee, and tossed their empty metals cups in the soapy wash water on the stand. Slocum got his buffalo robe out of the back of his supply wagon. He checked the loads in his Colt from the holster and the extra cap-and-ball .30-caliber model in his waistband. The second was a small gun, but it was effective at close range. Wild Bill Hickok liked that model. Said those big guns were unhandy and hard to get swung around when you needed firepower quick in your fist.

His foreman, Jim Lacey, came by. They shared a nip apiece off a good pint of Kentucky whiskey. "You four got it planned?"

"We hope. If I don't come back, it will all be up to you."

"You better come back, Slocum. These damn Indians have me upset."

"Hell, they may be like smoke in the morning—gone. They do that."

"And they don't, too."

"I'm going out the west way. See you, Lacey. Be back

about three in the morning, if not sooner. I plan to come back in one piece."

"Lots of luck."

"Thanks. I figure I'll need it."

Slocum left on all fours under the cover of the stinking, heavy hide. A rifle would have been nice, but he needed both hands to keep the buffalo robe over him. The skin would blend in better with the sagebrush than a blanket. He went a ways, then stopped and listened to the drums in the distance. They were having a big dance up there. Good. He and his men needed to get some of them eliminated to notch down their numbers.

In a short while, he reached a sandy dry wash and used it to go north. He paused every little bit to listen for any sound. Stopped, he heard one or more people breathing damn hard. He cautiously rose up some to learn the direction of all the private grunting.

Whoever it was, they sure were a long ways from their festivities. He climbed up the bank and kept low on the move with his Bowie knife in his fist. They weren't far over the lip, but he couldn't see them. Then he spotted a man's powerful bare back in a sitting position. There must be a woman under him. He heard her moans of pleasure, but no need in risking his self getting any higher. No way he could see her until he stood over them.

The man spoke in a deep bass voice, in the Cheyenne language. Slocum felt certain this man was a leader, extracting his pleasure from some squaw. He crept closer, concentrating on the man still seated on her belly, who rambled on unaware of being watched.

Then Slocum made his charge. His Bowie blade in a downward strike went to the hilt deep in the middle of the Indian's back, and a stifled scream died in his throat. The man pitched forward on top of the squaw under him. His knife had silenced the buck for good. It was her Slocum had to silence next. With a great effort, he heaved the Indian's thick body aside and caught her by her heavy braids before she could scramble away from him.

His other hand clamped tight over her mouth. Chills ran up the cheeks of his face. Naked as Eve, she was a slender-bodied young female and wild as any prairie chicken he ever caught under a gun-fired net. But he had suppressed her screams, for the moment.

"I'll take my hand away if you won't scream. Otherwise, I will gag you."

". . . you bastard. My father will kill you for what you have done to him and me." Her voice in a whisper, he figured she didn't want to be gagged.

"Darlin', he'd've killed me if he'd had the chance. What's your name?"

Her back straightened. "I am a Cheyenne princess. My name is Snow Flake."

"Mine's Slocum, Snow. I better get you back to camp. Who was he?"

"Bull of Thunder. My husband-to-be, of course." She was dressing in her snowy buckskin dress.

"Who is your father?"

"Man of Pipes."

"I've heard of him. Maybe, if he wants you bad enough, he might trade with me. Now, no tricks from you. Head for that ring of wagons."

"Are you the chief of those wagons?"

"I am." He took the man's ammunition belt to sling over his shoulder, and the buck's new Winchester. It was a much better gun than most of the men in his camp had.

Knelt down on one knee, with his left hand he wrenched the big knife out of Thunder's back and then holstered it behind his back. He wouldn't get much more killing done that night. But he did have a strong trade item—the chief's daughter.

On their approach to the wagons, Slocum alerted the night guards. "Hold your fire. It's me," he warned.

"Well, who in the hell is she?" a guard asked.

"Watch her," Slocum said, giving one of his men the rifle and ammo belt. "She's the chief's daughter. Her name's Snow. His name is Man of Pipes."

"Get any of them?"

"Her husband to be—he's dead now."

"What we going to do with her?" Kimes, the lead driver, asked.

Slocum frowned at him. "Quit licking your chops. She is damn sure not here for you to rape or torture. Anyone lays a hand on her, I'll cut that hand off. Am I clear?"

"Sure, sure, I was just asking."

"If she acts tame, let her loose. If she tries to escape, tie her up. You savvy that, Snow? Being tied up will hurt you."

She nodded and sat on the ground near the glowing coals that reflected on her light tan adolescent face. There was a cool night wind and the fire's heat must have felt good. Her husband-to-be lay dead. She must realize that her life would change quickly in the hands of her worst enemies, who had no respect for her rank.

Slocum went and looked for his foreman.

His man, Lacey, appeared sleepy-eyed when he joined Slocum, and he looked hard at her. "What did you fetch back?"

"The chief's daughter. We will have to wait to see how they react to our efforts tonight."

"She's a pretty good catch."

"I thought so. Her husband-to-be, who may have been a main warrior, is dead."

"We'll know something by dawn, won't we?"

"Yes. I don't want her raped or mishandled. Assign some men to be responsible for her. I told her as long as she didn't try to run off, I wouldn't tie her up."

"I can do that." Lacey yawned.

Slocum went off to find his bedroll to get a few hours of sleep before the others returned. On his back, under his soogans, he stared at the million stars. *Thanks, Lord, for another day . . .*

2

Lacey woke him. Kneeling beside Slocum's bedroll, his man spoke softly. "Everyone is back. They had some success."

"Good." Slocum threw back his covers and buckled on his six-gun rig while getting up. "Where are they?"

"Over at the campfire."

His boots pulled on, he said, "Better go see. How's my princess?"

"Wrapped in a blanket and sleeping, or playing possum."

"Good." He put on his hat as they hurried to the campfire.

"Anyone run off their horses?" Slocum looked the men over for an answer.

Joe nodded. "They won't have many to ride today. I scattered them best I could."

"I managed to send about three to the happy hunting grounds for good Injuns," the buck skinner, Johnson, said and spit tobacco aside. "That means there are considerable less to whoop around and shoot at us."

9

"We did well."

The sun had slipped up over the horizon when someone called out, "Hey, I think we have a deal coming. There's a buck with a white flag riding this way."

Slocum went to see who it was. Sure enough, he had a large white flag. No doubt a part of the bedding from some less fortunate settler that they'd killed. "I think we can do some swapping."

"Her, for what?" Kimes, his lead driver, asked.

"A ticket to get back on the road."

"You trust them?"

"About as far as I can toss them. Get me my horse and a rifle. I'll meet him."

"Be damn careful. Could be a plot to kill you," Lacey said and headed off to get him his needs.

Slocum studied the rider. Then he went over and shook Snow, still asleep under the blanket. "Get up, Snow. Who is this man out here?"

She wiped the sleep from her eyes, then hurried to her feet. For moment she stared at the rider approaching. "Little Bear."

"Good. Go back to sleep."

She frowned at him. "Why ask me his name?"

"When I call him Little Bear, he'll wonder how I know his name, won't he?"

She agreed and went back by the fire ring.

"Don't let her escape," he said loud enough over his shoulder. Then he mounted the stout red roan horse with the cropped ears that he called Sitting Bull. Rifle loaded and laid across his lap, he booted Sitting Bull out of the wagon ring to meet Little Bear.

They stopped thirty feet apart.

"How are you, Little Bear?"

The brave's eyes fluttered; he was obviously taken aback

by his name escaping a white man's tongue. "I come to ask if you have our chief's daughter."

"I have her and she's safe. No one will disturb her in my camp, or touch her. She is unchained on her word not to escape, so she is in no pain, nor will she be punished or threatened in my care."

"My chief, her father, asks for her back."

"Well, Little Bear, I figure as long as I have her, your war party won't attack my wagon train and we can go on to Montana. I have little to eat here in my wagons. They're full of of iron and wood to farm with. Nothing here that the Cheyenne can eat, wear, or care about. At the south end of the Crow country, I will give her back to you. But from here to there I will use her for safe passage. Little Bear, you will tell her father and your brothers they must come unarmed and take her home from up there. You have my word that she will be unharmed."

"I will ask him if that suits him."

"Take your time. Tell him she will be respected, but she is my pass to get that far north."

The brave stopped. "How do you know my name?"

"My God told me who you were."

Little Bear nodded and then spurred his horse away. Slocum smiled after him. That trick had got the buck just like he'd expected it would—a little confused.

Slocum rode back, handed a fledgling his rifle, and dismounted Sitting Bull. "Well, they are thinking about my offer."

"What did you offer them?" someone asked.

"To return Snow to them at the south end of the Crow land unharmed, if we are, too."

"Think it will work?"

"We have the ace in the hole, boys. That's her."

"Did you shock him calling him by his name?" Kimes asked.

"Maybe somewhat. But he damn sure didn't expect my terms either."

"What will we do next?"

"I plan to move out in the morning, with Snow riding up front with some of us."

"You're damn sure of yourself, is all I can say."

"We'll see."

Lacey joined him. "Yes, we will see. What about her for now?"

"Make someone guard her around the clock. She's our pass to Montana."

"I can do that."

"Good. We're less than half a day's travel from the river. We'll load up. She can ride with me and Johnson at the head of the line on a lead rope. We should get to the Tongue River by mid-morning to refill barrels and water this stock."

He went and found the new rifle he'd brought back and spent the rest of the day cleaning it. The renegades sent him nothing that day to answer his request.

The next morning, they ate breakfast before dawn and hooked up their teams of mules and horses to the thirty wagons. The animals needed some better graze and a belly full of water. The Tongue River bottomland could furnish both. They were less than a week from Billings, so Slocum hoped his plan worked. Johnson had chosen a horse and Texas saddle for Snow, and a rope lead to keep horse and rider safe and in sight. Her pretty brown legs were exposed in the morning sunlight. Slocum knew she could ride any horse this outfit had.

No sign of anything, but he gave Lacey instructions: If any Cheyenne showed up, Lacey and the wagon train should break off and make a circle out of the back half of the train. He gave the same order to Kimes in the number one wagon.

The animals were slow getting to a pace that he liked to see. Water and graze later would help fuel them for the next day.

The low sagebrush across the wide, flat valley couldn't conceal much. The Bozeman Trail wagon tracks ran northward and things looked clear. By Slocum's estimate, the line of tall cottonwoods along the Tongue was maybe a mile north.

Suddenly, two pistol-armed bucks jumped up from the ground in front of them, and it seemed they appeared out of nowhere. Slocum shot the one on the left in his bare chest. Johnson took two shots to stop his man. However, his horse shied in the process and he dropped Snow's lead rope. Quick as a cat, she stood in the stirrup, stretched over the horse's neck, and sought the lead. Slocum saw she had hold of it and he spurred Sitting Bull to catch her.

The race was on. She wasn't looking back, but her heels were working over the bay horse's side as she rode. Then, with a cross-over motion, back and forth with the lead rope, she began whipping him to run faster. Sitting Bull had his half ears laid back like he must have done this before. No doubt, many times, when his former Indian owner closed in to ride beside a buffalo and shoot him in the heart, behind his front legs. Inch by inch, he drew closer to being beside Snow.

No need to urge the powerful pony; he knew what was expected and was fast closing in. She swung the lead rope at Slocum, but he caught the collar of her dress, jerked her off her horse, and slammed her over his lap. Then he made a wide circle, slowing Sitting Bull down to a walk.

"No." She struggled over his lap as he held her in place.

"Catch her horse," he told Johnson, who'd caught up and reined his horse in.

"Any more sign of them?" Slocum asked.

Johnson shook his head. Then the buck skinner rode on

to capture the bay that had stopped a hundred yards ahead of him.

"What are going to do to me?" Snow asked in a small voice.

"I damn sure might spank you, when I get those wagons and horses to the river. I told you not to try to run on me, didn't I?"

"There was shooting. I was afraid."

"Two more licks for lying."

"You won't spank me—" She tried to look back to plead with him. He forced her down again over his lap.

"You disobeyed me. You have one coming and you'll get it when we make camp."

"Oh, don't spank me."

"You will be spanked when we make camp. You acted like a little kid running away when you promised me you wouldn't do this. I don't have time to mess with you now. I don't know if your relatives will try to raid us again, but they might." He stood in the stirrups to look across the flats—so far, no other sign of them.

"Let me up."

"You can ride right there all day. You disobeyed me."

"You are hardheaded."

"No. I didn't lie to you. You lied to me."

No answer. She squirmed some more on his lap.

"Be still." She obeyed him. No sign of any attack. But they now had fewer bucks to worry about than the number that had come to make war with them on the road the first time.

The wagon teams were coming at a jog in a long line and making lots of dust, but Slocum saw no sign of any Indians, either on foot or horseback. He short loped the roan for the river. They needed to be careful not to colic any of their animals once they reached the water. That would be all

Slocum needed at this point, so they couldn't let the thirsty animals over-drink at first and get bellyaches.

Snow beat on his leg. "I must get down. I must get down. I won't run."

With his hand full of her dress, he pulled her up and then gently set her down. On her feet, she nodded at him, looking very somber. He turned his head while she raised her dress to squat and relieve herself. Where was the war party? No sign of them. But he knew damn good and well they were still out there somewhere.

He spun Sitting Bull around, still looking for any threat. Nothing. He bent over in the saddle and swept her up on the cantle behind his back.

"Thank you," she said softly, seated behind him.

He never answered her, except to say, "Hang on."

With that accomplished, he set out in a hard lope for the river to be sure there wasn't a trap set up for them to run into there. She clung to him, but as an expert horse rider, she had no trouble riding behind him. The small river was in the open and hardly a place for anyone to be hidden. He slid Bull to a halt to look over all the country. Nothing was in sight. They could circle the wagons and water the animals here. There was also lots of graze to fill them up and rest them the balance of the day. That meant that in the morning, under guarded caution, they'd start north again, past the fatal Custer site and headed for the Crow reservation.

Slocum rode back and told Lacey to set up camp and have each driver water his horse with care and then graze the animal close by. Maybe Johnson and Joe could locate the renegades' camp and activities. A week or two and they'd be in Billings and could unload the freight. A week might be too stiff a schedule for Slocum to accomplish, but at most he was within two weeks of reaching his destination.

He met with two of his scouts.

"No sign of them." Johnson spit tobacco aside.

"You two can make some wider circles and look for them. Both of you be careful. We'll rest today here. Get our horses and mules healed, and I plan to start north again in the early morning,"

They agreed and left him to go on the scout. He rode around talking to his drivers, who were relieved they'd had no more attacks. Tough men, but also ready to deliver their loads and take a breather. Only a few of them bore minor injuries from the raid. His outfit was damn sure made up of tough frontier freighters, and they'd been tested over the past few days.

He motioned for Snow to slip off his horse at the main wagon. Lithely, she slid off Bull's rump and straightened her dress. Out of the saddle, Slocum stretched and reset his pants and gun belt.

"If you ever try to escape me again, I will bust your butt and keep you in ropes the rest of the time you are with me. Do you hear me?"

Subdued, she nodded. "I won't. I promise you."

"Well, you better remember it won't be a threat."

"Yes, I will. You have no woman?" she asked.

He shook his head. "No woman."

"Why not?" She traipsed along with him, her dress fringe whipping around in the strong wind.

"I don't stay long anywhere."

"She could not go with you?"

"White women like to be rooted."

He found his cook. "We'll be here until dawn tomorrow. Be sure they fill all the water barrels."

Jasper scratched his gray beard and used his thumb to indicate Snow. "Figure her kin left us?"

"I have no idea. I simply want to get up there and unloaded."

The older man narrowed his blue eyes. "Are we hauling stinking buff hides back?"

"If you want to be paid, I'd say yes."

The cook wrinkled his nose. "Even the damn food I cook will taste like that."

"Can't help it." Slocum shook his head.

"Yeah, yeah, but I need to complain to someone."

Two steps behind him, his companion was walking in his footsteps. When they left Jasper, Snow said, "These men complain like old women."

Amused, he nodded in agreement.

"What will you do next?"

"Make sure all my harness is in good repair."

"You must worry a lot to run this outfit."

"Yes. I have to." He glanced back at her. "What do you wish to do?"

"I would like to bathe in the river."

"That can be arranged. No tricks?"

"No tricks."

"Go bathe. But if you try to run again, you will live in chains."

"I have no soap."

"I have soap and a towel. Don't undress in broad daylight. White men don't expect that." He took her to the wagon and fetched out the two items for her. Then pointed to a less obvious site for her to go bathe. "Don't run away."

She agreed and set out for the point. Watching the fringe swish around her tan calves, he shook his head in amazement at how grown-up she acted for a mere teenager.

He stayed around the wagon and looked over his ledger book. All his expenses had been recorded so far as they should be. The return trip would be like Jasper had said. It would be a stinking long one, hauling those hides back to Omaha.

In a short while, Snow returned looking refreshed. He found her a brush for her hair.

"Water's cold?"

Busy pulling on the brush, she agreed with a small shake of her shoulders. "Very cold."

"I bet it was damn near icy." He chuckled. "I need to check on a wagon we've had trouble with. Come along, you can brush your hair down there."

She moved off the box she'd found to sit on and followed in his footsteps with the brush in her hand.

The wagon's hind axle was up on a jack and the wheel removed, with two men working on it.

"Is the situation better?" he asked them.

"We've greased it again. I think something is wrong with the axle. We better replace it in Billings," the bearded driver, Ivor Yankton, in his thirties, said.

Slocum agreed, "We can get it done up there."

"We'll keep greasing it till we get there. She your new pup?" He indicated Snow Flake.

"No, she is our insurance to get there."

The two men went on to a shoeing of some draft horses.

In his leather apron, sweaty-faced, burly-built Charlie McComb looked up from pounding the hot iron shoe on the anvil. "Getting a few of them shod today."

"Good. We move north at dawn."

"I'll get another team shod today."

"Fine."

His scouts returned with no sign of Snow's tribesmen near them.

"Will you shelter me from the Crows?" she asked when they left the two men.

"Yes. If your people don't come claim you, I'll take you on to Billings. I'll protect you."

"Good."

Slocum had no idea why, but the Crows were very separate from the other tribes. Some of them had been Custer's scouts, and that made the other Indians angry. The Crows, in turn, had shown their hatred recently by killing three major Sioux chiefs who were on their way trying to surrender.

Before the Little Big Horn, General Crook had gone to Nebraska to find some Sioux scouts. The Indian agent in charge at Fort Robinson hated the military and threatened the Sioux that if anyone went with Crook, his relatives would starve.

Crook knew the benefit of using tribe scouts, and he left there disappointed, without any Sioux scouts to return to Wyoming. The general blamed the lack of Sioux scouts for his own defeat at the Rose Bud Battle, only days before Custer's big mistake at the nearby Little Big Horn. Crook managed to get out of his entanglement and retreated back to Goose Creek.

"No need to worry, Snow, if your people don't come for you. You'll be safe with us."

She nodded that she heard him.

"Let's go eat. I hear the cook's triangle ringing."

She went with him. In line beside him, she took a tin plate and filled it, and then she sat on the ground at his side. She had taken a spoon to eat the buffalo stew with, but he noticed she hadn't taken any biscuits for herself from the large Dutch oven.

"You don't like bread?" He showed her one.

A slight frown appeared on her brow line, and she said, "I didn't see them."

"They are in that big kettle." He pointed out the open Dutch oven to her.

She set her plate aside and went over to get two. Once reseated, and after a bite of her first one, she smiled. "Good."

"Not bad. Not half-bad."

Then, like she'd forgotten something, she set down her

plate again, went to the fire, and brought back two cups of coffee for them.

"Hell, Slocum, she's handier than a pocket on a shirt," Kimes said, and stopped on his way past them to get an eyeful of her.

"Nearly so."

"She's pretty enough."

"Almost." Slocum watched for her reaction to his words.

Another frown, and then to hide her anger at his words she busied herself eating. He laughed, for he'd got her goat. That was all right; she could use some stand-down business. But she was actually the most striking-looking Indian woman he'd seen in years.

After lunch, he took her to Lacey, who was braiding some new reins for his own bridle. "Keep her safe. I'm taking a siesta. Any sign of trouble, wake me up. And kick anyone's ass that tries to mess with her."

"That could be lots of asses." Lacey laughed. He frowned when she took the braiding process away from him.

"It needs to be flat." Then she undid several braids he'd freshly made and sat herself down to fix it.

"You're going to get a lesson in braiding this afternoon." Slocum chuckled. *Show him how, pretty girl.*

3

Two days later, they reached the Crow reservation. No sign of Snow's people. Slocum had her ride in Kimes's wagon so she couldn't be snatched away by some young bold Crow buck. His outfit didn't stay at the Crow agency but went on upstream and camped. Jasper had some fishing gear, and he sent a couple of the younger ones with it to catch some trout. Then, with iron hooks baited with earthworms, they landed several fat trout.

They even gave an old begging Crow squaw a four-pounder to eat. She left them very happy.

About sundown, everyone ate a fried fish supper. Snow never missed a thing while helping Jasper fix it. While he worked at the other food, she took a sharp knife and cut out the bone, leaving boneless slabs of trout meat. At the same time, she studied how he cooked them. He'd have bet she could do just as good the next time by herself.

Jasper fried them brown in hot lard and made German fried potatoes and biscuits to go with them. Canned peaches made a fine dessert.

They all had enough of the meal that their bellies were too full. A meal like that was what made a man like Jasper more valuable than other cooks that were available.

After supper, Slocum sat on a crate, with Snow cross-legged beside him on the ground.

"Think you can catch fish now?"

She smiled with a nod. "I will have some iron hooks, too."

"They work good, baited with worms or grasshoppers later on in the season."

"Oh, yes, grasshoppers would work in the moon of the ripe chokecherries. I can see that. The oil to cook them must be hot. Real hot to make the trout brown. I saw that, too."

"If your people don't come for you, maybe you can become a wagon train cook."

He saw he'd needled her too much. She shed a few tears that she tried to hide from him. First time he'd caught her doing that. But she'd been his captive now for four days, going on five, and no sign of anyone to claim her. The Cheyenne would not come on the Crow reservation land to try to take her back, but in the morning his outfit would be headed farther north. No telling what would happen then. He'd expected a messenger two nights earlier to come get her— strange that no one came.

In the morning, after breakfast, they went on. She rode the bay horse by herself. She wouldn't run off in Crow country. From here on, she was simply nice scenery to have along with his crew.

They were all horny, as they'd been back in Fort Laramie, where some found pleasure in a nearby pig farm where cast-off prostitutes worked, or taken any available Indian woman among the post's hangers-on. The women at the pig farms were usually diseased, fat, and ugly, and some were even real old, plus there were always some crazy ones there, too.

But they welcomed the soldiers on paydays, or any other time they or anyone else had the low price they charged.

Billings would be next, though Slocum knew that while they'd been camped the night before, close to the Crow capital, some of his men had found flesh favors in their bedrolls from a few Crow whores that they slipped into camp or bedded outside the circle. He'd read somewhere that there was no more than one white woman to every ten white men on the Western frontier and that the commercialization of the oldest industry in the world—prostitution—went on wholesale everywhere.

But when the real women began to appear in the West, the war to ban their sisters of the trade became an outcry on every good woman's lips. Preachers who'd frequented such places of flesh in the past soon led the drive, with sermons from the pulpit that these daughters of Eve must be driven from among the Christian population of their towns.

They did so, even though the miners, ranch hands, and teamsters, who had no place in their lives for a wife, would thus be denied the friendly services of a dove, or any other female who understood them and knew their needs quite well. But so far the effort to bring about the demise of the flesh trade had been only a token one, as had the anti-whiskey forces' efforts to close down all the saloons.

Slocum saddled his horse after breakfast, and they brought a saddled horse over for Snow. Still no sign of her people, but they were still too close to the Crow, and he figured they wouldn't risk it. She joined him to eat breakfast, and her last guard made it clear to Slocum that no one had dared bother or even touch her during the night.

"Thanks, Jim," he said to the sincere young man. His mother had raised him right.

"How are you, Snow?"

"Better, since we are leaving the land of those Crow dogs." She made a visible shudder of her shoulders as they passed down the food line together.

He knew the Sioux and their allies—the Cheyenne, with the aid of their better-developed horse society—and others had pushed the Crow people off the buffalo-covered plains to the mountains. What one tribe called a section of their world had been stolen from another tribe. The Shoshone people had been pushed farther into the mountains by the Crow move.

Before the white man started west, the buffalo horse societies had had over a hundred-year span of their improved protein diet. So much so that their population soared. Once they got the Spanish horse, they no longer were cave people living in the Minnesota woods like the Sioux had been. With the horse and travois, they could follow the migration routes of the buffalo and eat hearty year-round.

Before then, Cheyenne and Arapaho people were dirt farmers in thatched huts along the rivers close to the Rockies. The horse made them mobile gypsies with tepees, and they became a part of the buffalo society.

At breakfast, Slocum and his crew ate oatmeal with bugs (raisins) and brown sugar. Snow delivered coffee in tin cups for the two of them, and he thanked her.

"How long will I stay with you?" she asked, seated again and ready to eat her cereal.

"Until I can get you safely back to your people."

"I will be patient. I am glad we are past the Crow."

"I understand."

"When will we be to this place you are headed for?"

"A few days. We're close."

"What happens then?"

"We'll camp and the men will let off steam, and I will try to find loads to go back."

"Will it be buffalo hides?"

"It could be. They have little else to trade or sell from up here."

She agreed and fell silent.

"It won't smell fresh, anyway," he said, teasing her.

"You are right. Will you ride up front today with me?"

"One of us will."

"I feel very secure riding with you." She waved her spoon at him.

"If I don't have any wagon trouble, I'll ride up there."

"Good."

"No one has threatened you or acted improper toward you, have they?"

"No."

"They shouldn't. I may find you a place to live during the time when we reach Billings. Towns like Billings have an edge of danger for Indian women, especially attractive ones like you."

"I can't stay with you?"

He shook his head. "Not all the time."

Five days later, they reached Billings and camped south of the Yellowstone River. Slocum left her in camp and sought his contact at the North Plains Implement Supply. The business was on the river, and no doubt when the flow was high enough they received shipments from low-draft riverboats coming up the Yellowstone.

Standing on the dock, his horse hitched at the rack, Slocum asked a broom-pushing swamper where he'd find Jerome Tinker. The man motioned toward an office.

He thanked him and strode over there. "I need to see Tinker."

"Yeah, well, who in the hell're you?" the burly clerk asked.

"My name's Slocum. I have a wagon trainload of farm machinery for him."

The man began to look through a wad of papers. "What company?"

"Charlie Hackett hired me. The papers are out at the wagons. Tinker was my contact man here."

The clerk never looked up. "He ain't here."

Slocum looked around at all the stacks of bales and boxes in the warehouse. "When will he get back?"

The clerk shook his head like he didn't know. "I found it. You were supposed to have delivered that in June."

Slocum shook his head. "I didn't get the job of ramrodding this train until mid-June in Omaha."

"Who in the hell needs mowers for the damn snow?"

"Mister, I did not order them. I only brought them here, and I'm damn lucky to have my scalp."

"I will need to see how this is paid for. Tinker won't be back for a few days. Don't ask me how many. He never said. Where are you?"

"Across the river. South. When can I check back?"

"Three days."

Slocum frowned at him. "Beat that. It's too long. I want to be headed south in a week."

"Hell, I can't do things just like that."

"You better. Or find someone who can."

Disgusted, he left the warehouse man, named Lonagon, and found a telegraph office. His wire to Charlie Hackett said he needed him to get these people off their asses and get him unloaded so he could head back. He signed it *Slocum*.

He told the man on the key he'd check back for the answer to his wire. Then he rode Sitting Bull back to camp, where Snow met him.

"You find the man?"

"He ain't there."

"Oh." The shocked look on her face told him she didn't understand.

"That's what I thought, too." He couldn't understand why they wouldn't take his freight. But he needed to find return freight and head that way, damn these pokey people. It was close to fall, and he wanted to have them back in Omaha before the snow flew. The plains between there and the Omaha plains could be bitter with cold and drifted in snow by November.

"What next?" Kimes asked, coming to find him. "Why in the hell can't we unload?"

"Lonagon said we got here too late."

"What are you going to do?"

"I may pile it at their doors. I telegraphed Omaha."

"Can I let part of the crew go into town?"

"Have them back in the morning, so if we can we'll unload and look for the freight going back."

"I'll divide the forces. She need a watchdog today?"

"Yes. I don't want anything to happen to her. She has my word."

"I'll be sure of that. Where are her people?"

"I don't know. They damn sure didn't show up to claim her on the south side of the Crow business."

"You may be stuck with her." Kimes went off laughing. "There have been worse things than that happen."

They replaced the wagon axle at a blacksmith shop. When they laid the new and old one side by side, the blacksmith showed them the crook in the old one.

"That's been what's wrong."

Slocum agreed. Replaced, they would have that worry fixed. In the return telegram, his man in Omaha said he could collect the charges, and for him to arrange to unload the wagons there. He also understood Slocum's concern about needing to return before winter set in.

Slocum stopped in the Elkhorn Saloon and drank a cold draft beer then picked at their free lunch counter. Fresh rye bread with sauerkraut and thin sliced corned beef stacked on it made a powerful good-tasting sandwich to match the beer. All he had to do was unload, find freight going back, plus return his captive to her people. All of it looked like a tremendous amount of work for one man.

After lunch, he told the hardware man, Lonagon, that he was unloading at daybreak and for him to have help and the doors open.

The man stuttered and finally told him he would do all that.

Slocum rode Sitting Bull out toward the hide yard and could smell it a block away. Mountains of buffalo hides were stacked all around the yard.

Charlie Griffin was the man in charge, and he shook Slocum's hand. "I heard someone with a wagon train just got here. You looking for a load going back?"

"I am, sir."

"Where you out of?"

"Omaha. That's where we headquarter."

"Can you get them there before spring?" Griffin asked.

"I can do my damndest. When will the first snow fall in Nebraska?"

Griffin blinked his eyes at him. "How in the hell should I know that?"

Slocum laughed. "That would tell you if I can deliver them or not."

"I figure over the winter this hide market price will break. A fall delivery would make a big difference in what I can get for them."

"I understand. I want to be back there, too. So we'll try our damndest to get back before the big snow."

They soon settled on a price for the hide delivery, with

fall delivery worth 25 percent more than a spring one. The contract gave Slocum something to shoot for. Plus, if they made it back early, he could skitter off to Texas and enjoy San Antonio's warm winter sunshine and all those fine brown asses that shook with their dancing and clacking castanets. What a wonderful place to spend the winter. Buried in a snowbank east of Ogallala would be the pits for him— better get unloaded and back on the road. The Alamo's bullet-pocked walls waited for him.

4

When he rode back into camp, his captive joined him. "You find a woman in town?"

He shook his head. "I was strictly on business. We unload and reload in the next few days. How many days is your camp from here?"

She turned up her palms. "My people have no home. Not since the Custer battle."

"We can look for them down where I got you. Someone will know where they went."

She blew her breath out. "Gone like the wind."

"If I can't find them, then you may spend the winter in Omaha." He about laughed at her pained face. "I'll need to leave you somewhere safe."

"Where will you go?"

"Texas."

"Why there?'

"'Cause I like it down there. It's warm in the winter, and they have pretty dancing girls as well."

31

"Oh."

He and Kimes talked over his plans to unload the train.
The hungover bunch in town would have to sober up fast,
for he had no plans to be snow- and ice-bound down on the
Platte River. His lead driver agreed.

In the night they took half the rigs to town, and at sunup
they began to unload them. Snow was with him, and she
watched the crates of mowing machines, strange racks of
rake teeth, and other equipment be moved inside the large
warehouse.

"What will they do with them?" she asked him quietly.

"Cut grass and stack it for winter. Then feed it next
winter."

She shook her head in disbelief. "White men look for
work, don't they?"

With a laugh, he agreed. Then he sent her to help the
cook, who was making lunch under less than easy conditions. He was fixing beef stew in a large kettle over a fire.
Versatile, Jasper made things work, and Snow could stir it
or help him get set up for serving it. Her being in the grum-
bling ex-noncom's company, there was less chance anyone
would touch her.

Lonagon and two of his clerks were marking off the items
unloaded. Slocum told Kimes and some of the others that
they needed to double-check that all items were marked off
as accepted. Some more of the "lost men" showed up for
lunch and fell into helping with the task.

By mid-afternoon, they had half of the wagons unloaded
and were ready to go back to camp. Lonagon looked on the
unloading as an overload for him, but he'd have an afternoon
to catch up on storing the stacks of merchandise on his docks.

Slocum took his prisoner back to camp. She craned her
head around a lot looking at the passing city life. She didn't
ask many questions, but he knew she must be confused as

to why people lived like this, all in one place. Back in camp, she hurried off to help Jasper, who was preparing supper.

The empty wagons were returning, and the rest would be off-loaded the next day with a full force of his men. Word was out that they'd haul stinking buffalo hides back, and no one was in a hurry to load them.

"Kency Holmes didn't come back," Kimes said to Slocum at supper. "He's a good kid. I don't think he'd quit us or got so drunk he couldn't come back."

"Anyone say where he was at last night?"

"Some tough bar down on the river. That was where they last saw him. The Tiger Saloon."

"Send some of his friends over to tell me what they know about it. And Buster Johnson, he can go with me to look for him."

Three of the younger ones were soon there, squatted on their legs, ready to fill him in on what happened.

"We never thought anything about it. He was getting in a heat over some breed girl that worked there. Her name was Pinky. We thought they went off together to do their thing."

"Yeah." The freckle-faced one spoke up. "Hell, when we were ready to leave we couldn't find him or her. No one knew where they went."

Slocum thanked them and turned to Buster Johnson. "You hear all this? That boy hasn't been heard of since then."

"Tough place." Johnson spat to the side. "Bunch of breeds and cutthroats hang out there. We can go see and maybe squeeze an answer out of one of them."

Slocum agreed and told his three scouts they were going to go look for Holmes. Horses saddled, the four of them rode into town, and Buster led the way to the saloon in shack town. Slocum had never been in this part of Billings. His men rode by the saloon and dismounted half a block away.

"Don't want them thinking we know too much about his last habits," Buster said.

Slocum agreed.

They went into the Last Draft first. It was practically empty, save for two skinny, ugly whores and a blinky-eyed barkeep who kept polishing glasses.

"He ain't in here," Slocum said, looking around.

"Who?" one of the women asked.

"A teamster works for us, named Kency Holmes."

"Never heard of him," the whore said. "I'd fuck any one of you for a dollar."

Buster shook his bearded face. "I won't give ten cents to see your asshole."

"Fuck you," she said sharply.

"I hope someone will," the old barkeep said, and they left laughing.

The Tiger Saloon was busier. A big card game was going on in the center of the room. Several drunks lay facedown on tables, passed out. Buster went around and lifted up fallen faces by their scalps looking for Kency. He made the circle and then shook his head. The bartender asked what they wanted. Slocum ordered four beers and paid the man. "Now, last night, Kency Holmes was in here. One of my drivers. He picked up a breed whore named Pinky. Where can I find either one of them?"

"I don't know any Pinky," the bartender said.

"Listen, big man, I've got a Bowie knife that will carve you up," Buster snarled at the man. "Answer the boss or you'll lose your balls."

"There ain't no Pinky works in here."

"Real easy, put that sawed-off shotgun on the counter," Slocum said to him. "We're all alive in here now. Let's keep it that way."

The bartender did as he was told and slapped his weapon on the bar, but his hand never moved to the trigger guard.

Slocum took the shotgun and ejected both shells out of the breech, pocketed them in his vest, and put the weapon back.

"Now, where is she?" Slocum asked the man again.

"Her lodge, I guess, down on the river."

"How can I find it?"

"Ask for her, I guess." The bartender shook his head. "I don't know shit about her."

"Any of those cardplayers know her?" Slocum gave a toss of his head at the card game.

The barkeep spoke to a man in the game. "Talbot, these guys want to know where Pinky lives."

The gambler turned and nodded at them. "Injun camp, big tepee with a buffalo herd painted on the side."

Slocum thanked him, then they drank their beers and left.

He felt grateful to be out of the Tiger's sour, smoky, stinking interior and on their way to Indian Town. Her tepee was easy to spot. Most of the camp housing consisted of buffalo hides tossed over round willow frames.

Slocum dismounted at the tepee site, and an Indian woman in buckskin rushed out the round opening of a door. He caught her by the scruff of her neck and stopped her. At the end of the struggle, he had her pinned facedown on the ground.

"I'm looking for Kency Holmes. He's a boy works for me who you screwed last night."

"Fuck you, white eyes. Let me up."

He pressed her down hard for an answer. "I need to know where he is."

"I don't know him."

Buster was there by then. He took her by her braids and jerked her to her bare feet. "You're too damn nice, Slocum. I'll get it out of her."

Without another word, he dragged her kicking and

wailing to the beach of the river and packed her out in the knee-deep water, clothes and all. He shoved her head under-water, and Slocum began to wonder if he'd drown her. But he jerked her up babbling, and she fought like a wildcat, though it was useless against his massive build and frame.

He doused her head underwater again. Her legs and feet kicked in the muddy sand until he pulled her back up. She'd had enough. Water running out of her mouth and nose, she gagged and tried to puke on Buster. At arm's length, it all went in the river, and her face looked bleached in total fear.

"Where is he?"

"Dead. In the river."

"Who killed him?"

"Two men."

"Tell me who."

"They will kill me if I do."

"No. I'll be first one to do that, if you don't tell me," Buster ordered.

"All right. All right. Britt Jones. Tom Hathaway."

"Where are they?"

"How should I know?"

He started to force her back underwater again, but she screamed out, "I'll tell you. I'll tell you. Beck's camp."

"Anyone know where that is?" Slocum asked the onlookers.

"East of here."

"Someone go get the crew. In the morning, I want every-one riding down the Yellowstone looking for that boy's body."

"What will the rest of us do?" Whethers asked Slocum.

"Take her along and go find that camp. I want those bas-tards that killed that boy."

"I'll go get the men," Whethers said. "We'll find his body."

"Tell Lacey we'll be coming back to help him look."

"I can do that, Boss."

Buster had Pinky on her knees on the grass. Her leather pants half-off exposed her bare butt, and Slocum could see that his scout planned to rape her. No need to stop him. He led Sitting Bull down and let him drink his fill. Behind his back, he could hear Buster Johnson's grunting.

How long since he'd been in bed with a woman? Way too long. This skinny girl here hardly appealed to Slocum, but his scout must really be enjoying her by all his noise. When Johnson had completed his task, she sat bare-assed on the ground, looking completely exhausted.

"Get your pants on," Slocum ordered her. "Show Indian Joe here where your horse is and get him."

When she made no move, Slocum threatened to kick her and she moved swiftly then to dress. "I do it. I do it."

She took his scout and went for a horse to ride. They returned shortly, with a thin horse wearing only a bridle. Grabbing a hank of mane, she lithely swung on his back and was ready to go. They moved down the trace along the river. Slocum saw no sign of any body in the fast-moving water beside them. He really hoped they could find that boy's corpse. Holmes needed a proper burial.

Past sundown, they reached the camp she'd spoken about. It was not a large one, and most of the inhabitants were at the large bonfire. Slocum made her dismount and go ahead of him.

Joe carried a rifle and Buster held his large Walker Colt .45 beside his leg. They walked a few feet apart from each other. At the fire, someone with a crock whiskey jug looked up. "Howdy, strangers. What'cha need?"

"Two killers," Slocum said quietly, and a wave of shock shone in the men's eyes. "Sit tight. Are they here, Pinky?" He indicated the circle of men.

She shook her head. "They have a small hut."

"Johnson, make her a torch. Don't anyone move. No need in anyone dying here. We only want two killers. Joe, watch them. Shoot anyone who tries to warn them or starts to leave."

With her in front carrying a torch, he and Johnson started across the camp.

"Think they're in there?" Slocum quietly asked when they stopped short of a shack. The light from her torch reflected off the closed door about twenty steps in front of them. He drew his Colt and cocked it.

"I'll kick it in. Toss in the torch and stand back."

At her hesitation, Buster wrenched it from her hand and joined him. Slocum's boot flung the door open, and that was followed by the blazing pitch torch tossed inside.

Screams of horror from the occupants followed shortly. The first out was a naked squaw. Buster caught her arm, flung her facedown, and told her to stay there. The first man to follow her Slocum smashed over the head with his pistol barrel, and he went down like a poled steer. The second one ran out, tripped over his partner, and fired his pistol. When he tried to rise, Johnson whacked him on the head. He was out cold, too.

The big man dragged both of them about ten feet from the burning building. Hugging her nakedness, the squaw joined them, sat on the ground, and looked back in distress at the burning cabin. The pair came to, groggy. While Slocum watched over the fire's bright scene with six-gun in hand, his scout went and found rope to tie their hands behind their backs. Both men must have slept in their pants, and they had no shirts on.

"These men are the ones that killed my man, Kency?" he asked Pinky.

She nodded.

"Did you drug him?"

"No, they jumped him when we were in my bed."

"What did you do?"

"Nothing. They stabbed him with their knives. I feared for my life, too."

"He didn't have any money. Why kill him?"

"Mean bastards."

"I guess so."

"What you going to do to us? You ain't the gawdamn law," the first man snarled.

"Yeah we are," Slocum said. "Judge rope's law."

The pair didn't say anything after that. Pinky found the woman an old dirty blanket to wrap up in. Then they made the two men walk barefooted back to the main camp and campfire.

"We need two long lariats to hang these bastards," Slocum told the men still at the fire. "For you that don't know, they killed a teamster of mine named Kency Holmes last night in Pinky's tepee. He was making love with her, and they stole in and stabbed him to death. No one kills one of my men and gets away with it."

Two ropes soon came for them to use. Slocum made hangman's knots in each of them. Within thirty minutes, chairs were kicked out from under the men and two pairs of bare feet hung two feet off the ground. The killers had gone to hell. Slocum and party started back for Pinky's place under the stars.

"You are damn sure tough men," she said to them.

"No, we're loyal men."

"That, too."

At noon the next day, they found Kency's bloated body in the Yellowstone, far downstream, in a quiet swirl out of the main stream. They wrapped his naked form in a blanket, and they had a funeral that evening at camp. When they finished his service, there weren't many dry eyes in the bunch.

Slocum gave the men two days' leave to blow off steam and for him to finalize his hide-hauling contract. They'd replaced the bad wagon axle, and all the wagon axles were greased and in good shape. Two wheel spokes had had to be replaced, and the harness was all well oiled and in good repair. The horses and mules all were sound and would be shod if needed. They were grazing some good forage and had gained some weight. Good enough. Two of his men wanted to quit, plus he had the vacancy of the murdered one. He planned to interview prospects for the job. There were enough unemployed men around, since the railroad construction coming that way had stopped over in Dakota due to a Wall Street bust.

Back at the wagon, Snow sat on her cot. "You found his killers and hung them?"

"Yes, we did. They're in hell. He was a good young man. They killed him because they were mean. He had no money."

"You have not found a woman to bed here?"

He sat down and shook his head. She knelt down and pulled off his boots.

"Why have you not found one?"

"Haven't had time."

"That is not the reason."

"Oh, what is the reason?"

Her smug smile gleamed in the light coming in the back donut of the canvas top. "You are too fussy about who you go to bed with."

"I might be." Her words amused him.

"Would you go to bed with me?"

When she finished stuffing his socks in his boots, he asked, "Would you like me to do that?"

She gave a small nod.

Gentle-like, he reached out and took her in his arms, then

stood to hug her. She held him and began to sob. With care, he reached down to raise her dress. Standing a little apart from her, he lifted the garment higher. She raised her arms until the dress cleared her body. He set it aside on his cot, then bent over to kiss her mouth.

His lips on hers shocked her, and she froze, so he stopped. "Relax, I can help you."

Then he kissed her again. She moaned softly as her mouth and tongue became involved. Her eyes fluttered shut, and long black eyelashes lay on her light brown cheeks. As their mouths grew more torrid, he began to undress. His shirt unbuttoned, he shed it. Then, unbuttoned and unbuckled, his pants fell. She gasped as if a stage curtain had been opened before her on a shocking scene. He stepped out of his pants and pressed her warm, supple body against his nakedness. Then he resumed kissing her and lifted her up to lay her on his cot.

Once there, she held her arms out for him to come down on top of her. With her knees raised and spread apart, he eased himself down between them. He entered her carefully, and they flew away to a raging sea of crashing waves, on the ultimate sex quest. Kisses fired them like Fourth of July rockets. Their movements drew them higher and higher, until the explosion blew out the fire and a gentle dive brought them back to numb reality.

"Why don't you have a woman?" she asked, still breathing hard.

"I have one tonight."

"Oh, you are more than any other man could ever be."

He sipped on her rock-hard nipples, and even in the dark wagon he could see her smile. She playfully wrestled his head back to her chest. What a lovely female. He felt jealous of the pleasure that her man must have taken from her. God made some women to be loved, and she fit that role perfectly. No restraint, no superstitions, no guilt—she gave her all to the last moment and beyond.

"What bothers me about you—"

"No, you don't know anything about me. I am a wanted man, and so I must change my job, identity, and location, without notice, to prevent my enemies from capturing me."

"I know places in western Montana and Idaho where no one could find us. Maybe they could find a tribe, but never find two lovers. Do you believe me?"

"That place must be heaven." He used his index finger to raise her chin and then softly kissed her lips. No place was safe. Wilderness or not, it wouldn't be trackless for men who were anxious to find him. He was better on the move than pinned down. Someday, some drunk would say, "Oh, I saw him in Billings on Sunday," and they'd rush to sniff out any trail.

"My dear, you are the loveliest woman in bed I could ever imagine." He kissed her and then started to get up.

"No, sleep with me."

He about laughed. "We won't sleep."

"Who cares? You have warmed my heart."

He gave up and lay back down, and took her in his arms to hold her. Hell, where else could he find such thrilling excitement? Her body felt so good to hold. *Go.*

They slept, mostly out of exhaustion, but periods of passion woke them, and they used each other's body to find more pleasure.

Before dawn, he discovered she was gone from his grasp and the cot empty. She'd gone to help Jasper prepare breakfast. He rubbed the back of his neck. What should he do with her? For one, she was too damn great to love to be anything but grateful for her presence and to go about his freighting business. Days were slipping by, and he didn't yearn to be snowed in on the way back. Dressed, he went for breakfast. With a plate of flapjacks, he found a place to sit on a crate, and she soon joined him after bringing them coffee first.

"How are you?" she asked quietly.

"I am fine. How are you?"

"Still excited."

"Oh?"

She looked around, then, seeing they were apart from anyone, in a low voice asked, "You are a real lover, is that the word?"

"You ain't half-bad yourself."

"When do you load hides?"

"Soon. I don't aim to sleep in the snow."

"Can I go along?"

He paused. "We'll see. You're a strong person, but you belong with your people. Mine are not nice to Indians, in places."

"Good, but for now I can go with you then?"

"I hope we make contact with them going south on the Bozeman."

"Maybe we will."

"Eat. I am going to buy you some clothes to wear today."

"I wish to please you until we must part."

"Hell, girl, you have pleased me."

They rode into town together. He went by and completed the hide hauling deal. If the Yellowstone River had been higher and shallow paddle wheelers had access to Billings, he'd not have gotten the hides to haul. But Griffin's desire to sell them in the fall set it all up. They would start loading in two days. Both shipper and hauler were to provide the help. Griffin looked out the window and smiled at the sight of Snow.

"Who is she?"

"A Cheyenne princess."

"I had an Injun wife—once, back a few years. Wildest piece of ass I ever had before or since. She wasn't that pretty, but boy she about burned my bedroll up every night." The hide buyer closed his eyes and almost shuddered standing there.

"What happened to her?"

"She didn't like living here. She wanted to live the Indian way, and I couldn't live in a tepee. I'd've been the laughing stock of the town. One day, she stomped her foot and told me if I loved her we'd leave here. I couldn't. That night she left me and I cried."

"You ever hear from her again?"

Sober-like, he nodded. "Her relatives told me she was killed later at Custer's battle. Probably fighting beside some of the warriors down there. Some women you just never forget."

"That's right. Thursday we load hides?"

"Yes. Would you sell her?"

"She's not mine to sell."

"Okay, I understand."

Slocum and Snow headed for the stores. He wanted her to have two dresses to wear when they headed on the trip south. The two ladies in the dress shop pulled the blinds when he told them he wanted two nice dresses made for Snow.

"What is wrong?"

"Don't be offended, but some of our clients might quit us if they learned we were making dresses for . . . an Indian."

He nodded. Snow understood English. He didn't have to tell her the story. She had her first lesson regarding prejudice among the white folks in the West. The women found two dresses in stock that she liked and that looked practical enough for her to wear. One was a blouse-and-split-skirt riding outfit, the other a long blue dress. The ladies promised to have them fitted for her in a day.

"Tomorrow evening about seven, can you come then?"

"Sure," he said, and Snow agreed

"Use the back entrance tomorrow night. Slocum, I have seen many women naked before, but she is the most beautiful girl I can recall. She is lucky to have a protector like you to look out for her."

"Thanks."

They left, and the shop was reopened. Slocum went for some things Jasper needed at the larger store down the street.

A clerk on a broom, busy sweeping, quickly confronted him. "We do not allow any fucking Indians in here. Get her out of here right now."

"Do you like living, boy?"

"Don't threaten me."

"Listen, wise mouth, she's with me, and if you don't like it, I'll stick a gun barrel in your ass and blow the top of your head off. Now stand aside. I have business to conduct, and she stays."

"What is happening here?" a smaller man wearing glasses asked, coming down the aisle.

"Mr. France, I told him he couldn't bring her in, and he threatened my life."

"Calm down, Johnny. We have a policy that no Aborigines are allowed in this store."

"She isn't that. Either you go back to the counter and fill my order or I'm skinning the hide off both of you."

France swallowed. "What do you need?"

"Baking powder, salt, ten pounds of sugar, and a little peace and quiet from both of you."

"Should I go get the marshal?" the boy asked his boss.

"It won't be necessary. Find his items and they will leave." The little man was near shaking at this point.

"You are damn right, and I won't be back either."

"I am sorry, sir, but I have to live here. If a lady customer comes in and discovers an Indian woman is in here, she won't be back."

"I'm sorry, too. I won't buy my wagon supplies here either, before I leave."

The boy came with the items, and Slocum reached in his pocket for money.

The man shook his head. "There is no charge for anything. Now, please leave before any of my customers come in and find her here."

"Suit yourself. Come along, Snow. There are other businesses in Billings need our trade."

Like a lady, she agreed, and heads high, they left the store.

He stopped on the porch and turned to her. "You see how they'd treat you in my world?"

"I do."

"Good. Let's go find a business that likes you and order what Jasper will need for us to head back."

She agreed. They rode down the street to the next large store. He motioned for her to go with him. She slipped off her horse. "Why should I go?"

"If he don't like Indians, I won't trade with him."

She giggled and shook her head. "They made you real mad."

No sign on the door mentioned it, so he started down the aisle. A big man in back of the counter looked at them. He wore a fresh white apron and looked the size of a gorilla that Slocum had seen once in a circus back in St. Louis.

"Morning," he said to Slocum, who nodded, and then he spoke to her in Sioux.

She shook her head, and he switched his greeting to Cheyenne. She returned his greeting.

"I think we can trade with him," Slocum said to her.

He stuck out a huge hand. "Why's that?"

"We got run out of a store down the street a few minutes ago, because of her."

"Oh. Maine's Mercantile?"

"Yes."

"He's a fussy old man. Me, I spent twenty years trapping up here and I knew them all. Folks don't like Injuns can go down to Maine's, but I've got better prices and I sell to anyone behaves their selves. I'm Big Jim Blazer."

"Slocum's my name, and I need some supplies to head the freight train back to Omaha. A barrel of flour, a barrel of oats." His list went on and on. Blazer wrote them all down and thanked him.

"I can deliver this day after tomorrow."

"Make it Friday. We load hides on Thursday."

"It will be there mid-morning. Where are you located?"

"Half mile south of the ferry. You have the list and I'll pay you then."

"Anytime. That squaw needs anything, you tell her she's welcome in my store."

"Thank you, Jim Blazer," she said.

"Oh, hell, she even speaks good English. You're a treasure, missy. You're a lucky man, Slocum. Ain't many can talk the language that good. None of mine ever could."

Slocum agreed, and with Snow carrying a sack of hard candy, they went back to the wagons. Most of the men were in town raising hell, knowing they had those stinking hides to load the next day.

When Slocum returned, several new faces were there waiting to ask him about a job. Some looked work-brittle to him; others were obvious drunks, others young boys. But from among them he hired three men who could harness a team with care and then drive them. He paid thirty and found, plus told them they were headed back to Omaha on Saturday. They were also to be back at the hide yard to help load the wagons early in the morning.

He wound up his hiring about suppertime and told the new men they could eat with the crew. At the setup, Snow brought him coffee after he filled his plate.

"Jasper laughed about the no Indian store."

"It wasn't funny in my book." Slocum shook his head, but she made him smile in the end anyway.

There was plenty of slow-roasted beef or buffalo piled on his plate, plus some small new potatoes, and he smiled. He recalled eating those first small potatoes as a boy on his home place. Damn, that had been a long time ago. A long time since he'd even tried to garden.

"You found the men you needed today?"

"Yes, Omar is over there. Simon is around here—somewhere—he has a scar on his face, and Tremel is the tall one with the golden hair. They can hitch and drive teams, and that is what I need."

She nodded, then asked, "How long to Fort Robinson?"

"A month. Why?"

"I just wondered."

"I need to find your people before then."

She nodded in agreement.

"Will there be people at Fort Laramie who know where your people are?"

"There might be."

There were many hangers-on, the tame Indians that camped around the fort and lived on handouts and trading. The year before, somehow, they had learned about the massacre, even before the first army dispatch rider arrived at that outpost to wire Washington with the news about Custer's demise. The Indians around the fort already knew what had happened and had fled, fearing reprisals against them. No one knew how they found out, but they knew about it and left, cautiously coming back only over time. After a year, the tame population in Indian Town was back to the same numbers as before the Little Big Horn.

Maybe Snow would find someone there who knew where her people had gone. He hoped they did better than that and found someone between Billings and northern Wyoming to get her safely home. Here he had this beautiful woman who filled his bed with her intent to please him and herself—and he needed to get her back to her own people. Tough deal. He already knew he'd miss her badly. So he better enjoy her body and ways while he still could.

That night in bed was even more spectacular than the one before. Their tryst reminded him of the fireworks at St. Louis the past Fourth of July, when the sorrow of the Custer loss had about smothered the nation's hundredth birthday. City officials had scheduled a great show and had fireworks on hand to set off on the shores of the big river. They decided, despite the nation's deep grief, not to deprive the children of the show. The huge display of rockets sent falling stars and lit the sky in patriotic colors for an hour. In the end, it was like a good funeral oration that uplifted the hearts and spirits of all the people who watched.

Slocum felt equally enthused about Snow's charm and exciting dedication to their lovemaking. Holding her smooth-skinned, muscular body tight to his own, he decided she was truly a star that had fallen into his arms. Damn, he loved her.

5

While they were crossing the Crow reservation, he made Snow ride in a wagon. He wanted no problem with a young Crow riding in and picking her off. Too much temptation there. Even wearing one of her new outfits, she still looked like a handsome Indian woman. The heavily loaded wagons lumbered along scented with the sour smell of the hides that caused a bitter taste in everyone's mouth.

Whiskey became a high-priced luxury to use as mouthwash, between the men who had any to sell and those without who wanted it. The smell of the green hides permeated everything. Even begging squaws along the way, when they caught the scent, moved back farther from the road to proposition the drivers by exposing their breasts or raising their dresses to show their hairy counterparts. Even with the language difference, the passing drivers knew what the women offered. Their asses—in trade for money or whiskey.

When they camped at night, Slocum told the men he'd fire anyone who brought one of the squaws into the wagon

51

circle. What they did out in the pines and sagebrush was their business, but none were to come inside the center.

He took Snow fishing away from the camp. They had cane poles and fresh red worms. The catgut line had a small lead weight tied on about eighteen inches above the baited iron hook on the end. The worm was cast upstream on about twenty feet of line and came downstream slowed by the weight. Trout were tempted to bite quickly, thinking the worm was free-floating from something the river had torn loose.

As their contest continued, lots of two- to four-pound trout were soon flopping on the bank. Then a big one took Snow's hook, and Slocum had to quit fishing and catch her around the waist before she was pulled into the swift water as she fought the big fish.

"Can we catch him?' she asked, with him holding her so she didn't get caught in the current and swept away in her zeal to land the trout. When the fish came up out of the water fighting the hook in his jaw, she screamed.

"Oh, I want him so bad," she cried. Her hands tightly gripped the pole, and the base of it stuck in her stomach as an anchor.

Slocum reached past her, still holding her waist with his other hand. He helped her hold the pole upright to keep the trout hooked. His hand could feel the muscled body of the large fish shaking his head "no" at her efforts.

By then, two teamsters had their shoes off and pants rolled up and were wading into the river to try to toss the fish on the bank. The trout came by, and Snow stalled him while one of the men threw him up on the bank. Others pounced on him, and she about collapsed with Slocum holding her up by her waist.

"Oh, thanks, all of you. He is huge."

They all admired him and agreed.

"Enough fish," Slocum said.

A little dazzled by the fight, she smiled. "The Crow have all the good land and big fish."

"Maybe you should marry one."

She made a bad face at him and shook her head.

Jasper, with his hands on his hips, studied the big fish when they laid him out on his fish board. "Why, little lady, you caught the fish of the year. He's big as them salmon comes up the Columbia River by the millions every year. I never seen a trout this size before."

The men ate him and the others in the fish fry that evening, and afterward many came by and told Snow she was the best fisherman they ever knew.

She beamed at them and shook her head. "It was only luck and you men with Slocum that saved me or he'd've drowned me."

That brought a laugh or two.

That evening on the cot, Slocum swam up her stream and they had much fiery lovemaking before they finished and fell asleep with her firm butt planted against his ripcord belly.

Each day was like a page in a new book for him. Soon, the hide smell became less noticeable. Miles rolled by, and they were past the Crows and headed south to Fort Laramie. No Indians threatened them, and several oxen-powered freighters passed. He paused to discuss conditions before them with the head man and to pick up any news.

He learned the army was paying the Sioux back with bullets for the Little Big Horn, and Sitting Bull was already in Canada. It was dry across the Midwest, and many corn crops had failed in the summer heat. Leaving the higher elevation where the nights at least had been cool, Slocum knew the trek east from Laramie would be a hot one until fall slipped in place.

Over the next few days, unusually heavy rainstorms swept off the Big Horns. Creeks swelled into rivers, and the earth turned to miring mud that sucked their wagon wheels under. The animals were soon in full fatigue, so they camped at Buffalo, Wyoming, to rest and hoped for a break in the torrents of rain and hail that persisted each afternoon. Slocum bought some grain for the horses and mules to help them recover.

His men had little money left out of their Billings pay to enjoy the treats of the town, and besides, the downtown was separated by the flooding creek that bisected it. The rain pattern appeared to be locked in on the region. People coming in from the east said it was like that clear over to Deadwood. Everything was mired in mud. Slocum had been there once for a spring thaw and knew how desperate it became crossing streets on two-by-six springy boards and not falling off them into the muck.

He'd bought a large used tent for them all to eat and congregate under. The men kept the tie-down ropes tight, and it withstood some tough gusts of wind. The hail size was too small to damage it. The Dry House, they called it, grateful to have shelter, and with their fingers nearly wrinkled permanently, having a dry place was wonderful.

One of his men, Omar Cone, broke his arm handling his team in the stopover, and the town doctor reset it. Slocum hired a wiry boy of perhaps fifteen, named Erwin Lynch, to drive, and promised his mother he'd pay his stage fare back home from Fort Laramie. By then, Cone would be able to drive his own team. The freckle-faced boy was excited and quickly showed his skill when they hitched up and headed south. As a regular farm boy, this double team business was no problem for him, and he fell into the job like a grown man. They rolled south in a letup of the rain and wound their way toward Fort Laramie.

Slocum met an army lieutenant named Franklin on the road south of Buffalo, and they talked as the train passed by. He and his company of cavalry were looking for some renegades bothering scttlers. The three Crow scouts eyed Snow sitting on her horse aside the passing train, but she ignored them.

"I haven't heard of any Cheyenne in the Big Horns. I would suspect they are out on the prairie east of here gathering buffalo meat for winter. We haven't found much sign of any. I think the ones who bothered the settlers were wanderers."

Slocum agreed. "A month ago, Man of Pipes's band attacked our train up by Winchester."

Franklin nodded. "I think they were run down by the army and are being taken to the Indian Territory."

"They were Man of Pipes's people?"

"Yes." Franklin swung his head at Snow. "She your captive?"

Slocum shook his head no and glanced over at Snow. No doubt, because of the noisy passing wagon train, she hadn't heard Franklin's words about her band being captured and moved. He thanked the man and rode over to join her.

He motioned for her to ride with him back to the front of the train. They short loped and arrived with Buster Johnson out front.

"What did he say?" she asked when they settled down, riding at the head of the train.

"He said he thought your band had been captured and they would be moved to the Indian Territory."

"Man of Pipes's people?"

"That's what he said."

She looked shaken by the news. "Where is this place?"

"Many miles south and east of here."

"Does he speak the truth?"

"I can learn that at Fort Laramie."

"What will they do at this new place?"

"Farm."

She made a face. "My people are not farmers. They are warriors and buffalo hunters."

"There isn't room for them out here."

She nodded, crestfallen. "The white chief has decided our fate?"

"Yes, be farmers or die. The Big Horn fight only quickened their process to put all Indians on reservations and make them farmers."

"I was not there. I only heard stories from some of my band who fought there."

"Was your man there?"

"Oh, yes. He said it was a great day for our people. The guns of the yellow legs were silenced, and they would no longer be able to fight us."

"Did he not know they were only a small piece of the army?"

"I don't think so. The men returning were so excited. They had stopped a large band of soldiers and silenced them."

Slocum nodded. "We can learn the truth of this story at Laramie. But I have not heard or seen a sign of them since I kidnapped you."

She nodded. "What is this place like where they will send us?"

"Hotter than the mountains you like."

"There are no mountains there?"

"None."

"Water?"

"More water, but no clear trout streams."

She shook her head, tossing her thick braids. "Sounds like the hell in the preacher's book."

Slocum chuckled. "Well, you will see if it is like that when you get there, huh?"

She looked downcast.

"One thing, neither you nor I can help them. Brighten up. You still have many miles before you face any more decisions."

"I will try to work harder and lose myself in helping Jasper cook and feed the men."

"They enjoy you."

She shook her head. "They treat me very nice. I feel I am among friends."

"You are."

Days were long, and afternoons they stopped so the animals could graze and get ready for another hard pull the next day. Some men took naps. Others repaired harness or wagons. The scouts shot a buffalo every few days, and they were butchered and the meat brought back to camp. The men ate hearty meals of buffalo meat roasted over fires, stewed in vegetables from the garden of a homesteader's wife they traded with, providing staples she needed or paying her in cash.

There were few fusses among the men. Slocum, like a sea captain, nipped them in the bud and separated the combatants with strong words. That chore as a leader was ever present when working single men, and Slocum had a good handle on the matter. He'd also buffaloed the ones he considered the tougher bullies into minding their own business or getting to walk home.

He spent his days keeping an ear out for any problems. His bed partner said little about the movement of her people and worked hard helping make meals and washing dishes and pots. Jasper considered her an angel sent to help him.

She and Slocum were in bed one night after enjoying the

pleasures of their bodies. "Are you going to leave me in Fort Laramie?"

He kissed her proud nipple and smiled. "That's up to you."

"What will you do when you reach this village where the wagons belong?"

"Omaha?"

"Yes." She wormed her nakedness suggestively against him.

"Oh, you are a thrilling woman, Snow. You spoil me. I won't stay there long."

"Good, I enjoy you, too."

He kissed her again, and they went back to making love.

The next day, wheels rolled and a cold rain moved in again. Noontime, the large tent was put up, and everyone without a slicker was soaking wet. They started a fire to dry them out, and Jasper and Snow began the evening meal preparation. On the side of his preparations, he put her to making donuts they called bear tracks.

As the hail popped on the tent's roof, she was the center of attention. With a long fork she raised each donut from the boiling grease and let it drip a little, then put it on a plate held out by a teamster. When the giant fry pan was empty, she reloaded it with the next ones.

Everyone stood patiently in line, waiting for her to cook the next batch. They teased her some, but all good-natured.

"Do squaws do that at your camp?" someone asked her.

"They would if they knew how and a white man furnished them with an iron pot like this and the lard," she said.

One wise guy in line said, "I'd furnish it, if you'd marry me, Snow."

She shook her head "no" and stirred the donuts. Amused, she waved her fork at them. "I don't want to be your wife."

"Aw, we'd spoil you."

She waved them away and turned the donuts over. They were close to cooked.

Those forked out, she started anew on the next batch. A fresh set of wise guys teased her.

That night on the cot, she shook her head. "Those men could eat a ton of those bear tracks."

"And flirt with you." He kissed her, then fondled her hard breasts. The two of them quickly built up steam to join each other's body. She spoiled him. As he entered her and she softly moaned, he knew every man in camp would have given an eyetooth to be in his position. Then they were swept away in passion's arms and heavy breathing to a whirlpool of fire and, in the end, exhausted relief.

Travel was good the next day. They reached Fort Reno. There was water and good grazing. Slocum told them they could rest there for a day or so. His farrier wanted to re-shoe some horses, and the draft animals could rest after the long pull. They would soon be at Fort Laramie and then turn east.

He made half the force stay in camp and guard the herd. The other half had a day off to wander over to the fort, drink some liquor, screw a whore that hung around there, or simply sleep. Some did that under the big tent. One driver set up a folding chair and began cutting hair outside the tent. And did lots of business.

Slocum's scouts had brought Jasper a fat buffalo carcass, and he hung it in a wet canvas wrap so the evaporation would cool it. The boys who helped had to carry buckets of water from the Laramie River and keep the carcass wet so it cooled.

Slocum and Snow saddled up and went to the Indian village east of the fort to talk to the blanket-ass crowd about where her people might be.

"Took . . . them . . . in many . . . wagons to place of

Indian gods. They won't go to Indian Territory until spring."
The old Indian's halting speech was enough for Slocum.

"They are over in the Black Hills," he said to Snow.

"How far is that away?"

"Maybe two hundred miles."

"Could I go there?"

"It won't be nice. Winter is close. Those people will be exposed, unless they have barracks built for them."

"I might be able to help them."

"They also may be miles from there. All he knows are rumors. At Fort Laramie they have a better telegraph connection, and when we get down there maybe I can find where they are."

"They have one here." She made an impatient face.

"It hardly works, getting through. Down there we can wire the Department of War and find out where they are."

"We'd be farther away then, too, wouldn't we?"

"If we went to find them, they might not be anywhere we look. Wait until we can get dependable contact and we know for sure what the army's plans are for them."

"I am impatient, aren't I?"

"Yes, but you're cute, acting like that."

She wrinkled her nose. "You are a hard man to figure out. Maybe we should go to your cot and see what happens."

He looked around. Clouds were gathering and it would probably rain that afternoon. Good, they could work this out with her on her back. Suited him fine.

And they did that very thing in a fiery fashion in their bare flesh.

Small hail pecked on the tight canvas cover over the wagon's hoops. Slocum squeezed the cheeks of her small ass and let fly inside of her. Then they kissed like hungry wolves and slept wrapped together as the deluge ran off the canvas sides. He wasn't interested in giving her up. But he knew that day would come. Oh, hell, he would miss her bad when she left him. *But that was his life.*

6

Someone outside called his name. "Slocum. Slocum. I need to talk to you."

"Coming." He laid a hand on Snow and told her to stay, that he would see what they wanted. Quickly pulling on his pants, he moved the flap aside. "What do you need?"

"Some guy shot two of our men in a fight about thirty minutes ago in a saloon in town."

"Are they hurt bad and who shot them?"

"Bad enough. He got away."

"Aw, hell. Saddle my horse and I'll go see what happened." He turned back to Snow while the man ran to get a horse for him to ride. "You stay here. You're safe in camp. I'll go see what the hell happened down there and be back when I can." He buttoned up his shirt and tucked it in. She handed him his gun belt and he kissed her for doing that. Then he swept her up and kissed her hard.

"I'll be back in a little while," he promised, then pulled on his boots and put on his slicker.

One more quick kiss and he climbed out of the wagon. Two more drivers on horses were bringing him Sitting Bull on the run.

Once he was mounted, he rode up to the canvas donut in the back of the wagon cover. "Give me the rifle, Snow."

She had on one of his shirts and smiled when she handed out the long gun. "I will be here waiting."

With thanks and a wave of his gun, he reined off to join the others. The men led the way, and once in town, Slocum saw the crowd in the street before the false-front saloon. He and his men reined up, and Slocum dismounted and waded through the crowd.

"What happened here?" he asked the noncom in uniform who looked to be in charge.

"Had a shooting, best I can tell. Those two your men?" He pointed across the room.

Slocum saw Arnold Beavers and Harold Sorrel both bandaged up and the doc working on a third.

"Two I can see are. Why?"

"They said some cardsharp was cheating. There was a scramble for guns. The gambler shot them both with his two-shot derringer, then shot that last guy with a .30-caliber Colt from inside his coat. He raked up all the money on the table and headed for hell knows where."

"He have any backup?"

Arnold shook his head, holding his bandaged arm. "Sumbitch was damn sure quick with that little pistol."

"What did he look like?" Slocum asked, not worried about his fast draw.

"Forty years old, white sideburns, blue eyes, thick mustache."

"He talked like he was from back east. He damn sure ain't Southern." Harold looked like it hurt him to even talk.

Slocum turned to the men who had brought him there.

"One of you can learn the direction he went, one of you go back to camp, send my scouts in here. Tell Snow I went to find this shooter and tell Lacey to watch her till I get back."

"Come on, there's a horse taxi out here," he said to the wounded pair. "Jasper has some painkiller. He'll take care of you. How much money did he get?"

"We didn't have much, but the other guy he shot had a few hundred on the table."

When he looked over at the wounded man, Slocum saw he was too bad off to talk to. The doc was still working hard on saving him.

Slocum spoke to the bartender next. "What happened?"

"Someone won and that gambler flew off the handle, went to cussing and used his hidden pistols on those two, then he dropped them and drew a .38, shot the other guy. His name's Don Ackers and he owns several ranches and businesses up here."

"What made him that mad?"

"I don't know."

"He ride in on a horse?"

"I think he stole a cowboy's horse out there at the hitch rail." The barkeep shouted at the three men on the end of the bar. "Did he get one of your horses?"

One of them answered, "Yeah, and my saddle, too. He's a watch-eyed bay horse. Gelding, about six years old. Has a YX brand on his right shoulder. That saddle was made in Texas and cost me two months' pay."

"What way did he ride?" Slocum asked

"West."

Slocum shook his head at the man. "Big help. I never met him on the road coming in."

"He rode off to the west. I saw him."

Slocum turned to the bartender. "Give me a beer. My scouts will be here shortly, and they can track a pissant."

"Get a sandwich over on the free bar."

The man served him a foamy mug, and Slocum took it to the free lunch counter. There was lots of coarse bread. He chose the rye bread, cheese, sliced ham, and put some mustard on it. The first bite was good.

A town marshal arrived in his black suit and tie. "What the hell happened in here?"

"They took the worst one up to Doc's," the bartender said. "They stole that cowboy's horse and saddle."

"Who did it?"

"Hell, ask them. He must be halfway to Montana by now," the bartender said.

"Listen, I can pull your damn license in one sweep of my pen."

"Do it. See how long you wear that badge. These men know what happened. Ask them."

The marshal stepped over to where Slocum stood eating his sandwich. "What do you know about this?"

"He shot two of my teamsters. The doctor treated them and I sent them back to our camp. My scouts are coming. You don't shoot my men and get away with it."

"This is a matter for the law to handle, mister."

"The sumbitch rode off with that cowboy's horse. How're you going to get him back standing here?"

"I'll put a wire out and they will get him."

"Yeah, that will really help." Slocum shook his head in disgust and took another bite. The man was crazy. He hoped his scouts came soon and that they'd learn where the gambler went. The law wasn't about to apprehend him. He finished the beer and put the mug on the bar. The lawman had gone outside, and when Slocum stepped onto the porch, he was chewing out a person on the boardwalk.

His sandwich consumed, Slocum went across the street

and spoke to an old Indian sitting on the ground. He squatted down on his haunches. "Chief, you speak English?"

The man nodded.

"The man who ran out and stole the watch-eyed horse, where did he go?"

The old man leaned forward. "That way. Him turn at second street and go north."

Slocum gave him three quarters and thanked him. The wrinkle-faced old man smiled at his reward. Then he sat back and closed his eyes.

Hearing riders coming, Slocum went over to his own horse. He swung into the saddle as they reined up.

"Where's the shooter?" Buster asked.

"He rode a stolen watch-eyed horse, went west to the second street and turned north."

They nodded and hurried in that direction. The gambler must have gone toward the Bozeman Trail. The four charged up the street, headed north. On the way, they stopped several men on the road and learned he was an hour or so ahead of them. No surprise to Slocum.

He and his men pushed their horses. They had four hours left until sundown. To close the gap, he kept the horses in a long trot, and they reached a fork in the road. Johnson pointed east and they followed his lead. The team split up in the small settlement they came to, to see if they could find the gambler and the horse. Indian Joe whistled, and they all tore out to find him on the north side of the cluster of buildings.

Slocum reined up and saw the man holding a pistol to a woman's head and dragging her out in the yard of a house.

"She'll die. She'll die."

"Put the gun down," Slocum ordered. "You kill her, we'll kill you in less than thirty seconds."

"I'll kill her, if you don't drop your guns."

"We aren't going to do as you say. Drop your gun."

"Please, mister, he'll kill me," the woman cried.

"Take that gun off her." Slocum kept coming

"I'm going to kill her, if you come one step closer—"

Slocum shoved the kidnapper backward, and the woman broke loose. The pistol went off in the air. Slocum got hold of the man's gun-hand wrist and carried him to the ground. From on top of the man, he wrenched the revolver from his hand. His men helped the sobbing woman to her feet. Whethers brought a rope to tie the captive's hands behind his back. They soon had him trussed up and facedown on the ground.

"Slocum, you had lots of nerve taking him on," Whethers said.

He shrugged off the comment. "He wasn't going to shoot anyone."

"He shot those boys of ours."

"Where he wounded them wasn't where a real killer would have shot them."

"What do we do with him?" Buster Johnson asked.

"He's a damn horse thief."

"I'll make a noose."

"Good. There are some cottonwoods up the valley. Whethers, get the money he has on him. Most belongs to the man he shot, is what I understand." Then Slocum removed his hat. "Did you know this man, ma'am?"

"No. He busted into my house."

"He tell you anything?"

"Said he was on the lam and I must hide him. I was so scared I am still shaking."

"I am very sorry, Mrs. . . . ?"

"Mrs. Kelly. My husband is up in Nebraska. He's a freighter."

"This man won't ever bother you again. I promise you, Mrs. Kelly."

"Could I thank you? I thought both of us would die in my yard."

"No need. He shot two of my men back by the fort."

In a small voice she asked, "Could you hold me, so I stop shaking?"

"Yes."

"Let us go inside, so gossips don't see us."

He had to duck his head to enter through her low front door. There was a kitchen chair lying on the floor. Otherwise, it was a neatly kept house. In his arms, he could feel her trembling.

"I'm sorry that he picked on you to scare."

"Oh." She shivered as he held her tight to him. "I don't know what I will do. Kelly won't be back for several weeks."

"I can stay awhile, if you want me to."

"I feel much more secure in your arms. Please stay."

"My men have work to do. Excuse me for a minute?"

"Surely."

Buster had the prisoner on a horse, and the others mounted up.

"Return the money to the man at the doctor's or to his family, and return the cowboy's horse. She's very shaky. I plan to comfort her for a while. Meet you later back at camp."

"She's very upset," Johnson agreed. "We can handle this."

The three men nodded.

"Your horse is in her barn, unsaddled and fed," Indian Joe said. The three scouts rode off.

The sun was setting as they headed for the cottonwood gallows. Slocum stepped back inside, and Mrs. Kelly hugged him with a shudder.

"What will they do with him?"

"He's a horse thief. The law says hang him."

"I understand."

He closed the door.

"Are you married?" she asked.

"No."

"I would hate to . . . force you to do anything against your beliefs." Tears spilled down her face.

"You won't do that."

"Take me to bed then. Maybe there I can forget this whole thing. I am sorry I'm so reckless, but ten years ago, some Sioux bucks captured me. They were on the move, and I rode on my belly over one of their horses a very long ways. Some brave men intercepted them and rescued me. I was shaking this bad that night. One of the men took me to his bedroll and engaged me in sex and I recovered. I don't cheat on Kelly, but in this case even he would agree—I need some relief." She clenched her teeth and quaked under his hands on her shoulders.

"We can do that. Should I undress you?"

"Help me, please."

He bolted the door and turned back to undo the buttons down the front of her dress. They were small buttons and many. She undid his gun belt and hung it on the ladder-back chair she had set back up. His hat she put on the other chair post.

The dress unbuttoned, he pushed it off her shoulders and slung it on the table. Next, she undid the waist and took off some of her slips. She stood in a thin slip that went below her knees. His boots toed off, he started on his shirt buttons. She helped, and he had to stop to hold her until she quit shaking so hard. Finally, he was undressed. Covers thrown back, she went to the bed, climbed under the sheet, and pulled it up to her neck.

He lifted the sheet and slid in beside her. Under the covers, he moved her slip up over her waist. He guessed her to be in her late twenties. When he pushed the slip up over her pear-shaped breasts, her entire body trembled under his hands.

With eyes squeezed shut, she held her hands at her sides closed so tight her knuckles were white. He rose to his knees over her and kissed her lips, but she didn't respond. With care, he gently moved her legs apart and climbed between them. Her trembling body shook the bed. His tool nosed gently into her, and her mouth opened. His slow application of force increased her breathing, and then her knees rose to help him. Her arms went around him and she pulled him down on top of her.

He was concerned he might mash her as their bodies melted into one. She turned from a numb, trembling body into a hot lover and wanted him as close as she could get him. It was a fiery match that made the bedsprings creak and went on and on, until in the last flaming moments they collapsed in a pile.

"Thank you."

"I don't want you relapsing." He noted how calm she had become and the faint smile on her face.

"I suppose. We could do it again."

He kissed her until they were off again. This time, she kissed him back, and they had an even wilder session that almost made the bed smoke. In the end, he kissed her and reluctantly climbed out of bed and dressed. She wrapped herself in a sheet to trail him to the front door and thank him for his tender feelings for her.

He kissed her good-bye, then went to find his horse. In the saddle on Sitting Bull, he paused by the yard fence covered in vines. She stood on the porch with a shawl around her. He gave her a nod and she returned it. Then he loped Bull off toward the cottonwoods and the Bozeman Trail.

His wagon train waited for him. He rode by the hatless, silent, horse thief with his stocking feet two feet off the ground and a knotted noose beside his left ear. He'd never steal another one, that was certain.

Slocum was back to the wagons before his scouts got back. The two wounded men were sleeping. His man Lacey met him.

"You find him?"

"Yes. The scouts took the money back to the worst injured man and the horse back to the cowboy. They'll be along."

"Our two men told us what he did. Did he give you a fight at the end?"

"No, he hid, using a nice lady as a hostage."

"Snow has food for you." Lacey nodded. "I imagine you're tired?"

"I'll be fine." Snow came over with a plate of food, and he hugged her.

"I am glad you are safe," she said.

He sat down on a crate and took the plate of food. She gave him a fork and knife. Pleased to see her, he smiled and took them. "Thanks."

"Anything else happen?" he asked his man.

"I'm wondering how those two will drive their teams," said Lacey.

"There are some helpers can drive them, or the scouts can, until they heal. We're far enough south we should be safe from hostile tribes attacking us."

"I imagine we can do that."

"Tomorrow, we'll start south again. Winter's coming."

Lacey agreed.

Slocum knew his man had no wish to winter the wagon train in the deep snow of middle Nebraska. They still might make it unscathed back to Omaha. He planned it that way. In a week to ten days they'd be in Fort Laramie. Then they'd turn east on the worn path back to the big city on the Missouri River.

That road was a strip of land depleted by all the western-bound settlers' wagon trains. Feed would be short on this route and firewood impossible to obtain. The westbound traffic had stripped the country of both grass and fuel for almost a ten-mile swath from Omaha to Fort Laramie. Slocum could recall the once seven-foot-tall prairie grasses that had to be cut so the surveyors could lay out the train tracks. Those plants no longer existed—wiped out by feet and time.

In places, he'd be forced to cross the Platte and take less-used routes that paralleled the river over there. The flow was low this time of year, but it still required lots more work to switch sides. If the renegade Indians weren't bad enough, he still had to get the train back and Snow back to her people.

Later, when the two were in bed, she asked if he was too tired to make love. He laughed. "Why, not for you, girl."

He gathered her in his arms and kissed her with all his effort. No need to let her down. She expected his attention. It was up to him, and he knew how.

7

They finally reached Fort Laramie, a hot, dusty place, in early September. They camped out on the Laramie River, where there was better feed for the draft animals, but they had to bring them back to camp each evening. Slocum set up guard duty, for at this point horse thieves would be the greatest danger. No one wanted the stinking hides; there were plenty of them out there anyway. He told the boys herding the stock to keep moving them to better feed.

He and Snow rode into the fort. He intended to talk to the commander and secure any information he might have on where her father and the rest of the band were being held. So that the authorities couldn't arrest her, she stayed with some tame Indians he knew until the meeting was over.

A few hours later, post commander Colonel Anderson allowed him a meeting. "What can I do for you, Slocum?"

"Colonel, I understand the Cheyenne band of Man of Pipes is being held through the winter at the Sioux Agency or Fort Robinson before being taken to Fort Reno in the Indian Territory. Is that the plan for them?"

"I think that's the plan. They gathered up about seventy-five individuals—men, women and children—and took them over there before sending them south next spring. They have the reservation set up near the fort. I don't think the Cheyenne will stay down there, but if they try to run, they will be close to a military facility."

"They won't get down there next year until it's too late to plant food."

Anderson stood and looked out the window at the marching field. "Obviously, you know that. But we have gotten so much bad publicity over the years about moving aborigines in the wintertime, I'm certain that's why they won't move them until the spring thaw."

"Thank you."

"Do you have a case of losses you wish to charge them with?"

"No, sir. But I spoke to a tribal member who wishes to return to his people. He sent me to ask if they would be there, if he went there this fall."

Anderson nodded. "They are there for all winter. Supplies have already been hauled up there to feed them."

"Thanks."

Anderson turned to him. "Will your friend go up there and join them?"

"I think he will. Yes, he plans to. Thanks again, sir."

"You're very welcome. He must be a real friend to send you here to ask me."

"Yes, he is. I was concerned for him."

"What are you doing here?"

"Freighting hides back to Omaha."

Anderson nodded that he understood. "Have any trouble on the Bozeman?"

"Yes, that band struck my train, but they lost more than we did."

"Have a safe journey. We need more tough people like you."

Slocum recovered Snow from the tame Indians, and they rode back to his camp.

"What did you learn?" she asked, riding beside him.

"Your people are at Fort Robinson. That is a large Sioux reservation of Chief Red Cloud. They will be there all winter. They already have food supplies up there for them. In the spring, like I said, the army will take them to the Indian Territory near Fort Reno."

"That makes me sad. But you were brave to go ask about them."

"He wouldn't eat me."

She laughed, but traces of tears were on her lashes. He rode in close, leaned over and kissed her. "Don't cry. You're a brave young woman."

"Thank you, my big man. Could I go there myself and join them?"

"No. You might get harmed. Lots of cruel people there who wouldn't respect you."

"I am happy riding with you, but I really belong with my people."

"Good. Now we know where they are and will be, I'll find a way to return you to them."

"Good. I know you have been concerned and I thank you."

"No, you're such wonderful company, I'll hate to lose you."

"That's good."

They topped the rise and saw smoke. It was a prairie fire on a wide front. The wagons sat right in the path, and the horses to pull them out of the way were off somewhere grazing.

"I better get down there and do something." He set heels to Sitting Bull, and they raced for the wagons. The camp was set up close to the river, but considering the direction the fire was coming from, it would be no barrier to it.

He slid Bull to a stop and leaped off. "Get some buckets and wet down the grass south of the camp. We'll need to set a backfire to stop that fire from burning us down."

Men standing with wet burlap sacks dropped them and went to dipping water out of the barrels and throwing it over the nearby grass on the approaching-fire side of the camp.

The dark, billowing, ominous smoke and five-foot-high flames were coming fast on the wind. Lacey joined him, trying to get the grass past the wet spots to burn.

"Snow, go get a dry burlap sack and some kerosene. This is way too slow," he shouted.

Lacey agreed and said, "I'll get a rope to tie it on."

"Right." Slocum squatted on his boot heels and cupped the small blaze he was trying to start in some dry bunch-grass. The task was too slow. Maybe his fire drag would do the trick.

Someone brought his saddled horse. He undid the lariat, and Snow arrived with Lacey and tied the sack on his rope.

"Now, this may start more fire than we need. So have the men ready to beat that out on the start—we need a dead zone around us."

Lacey and Snow agreed with him, and she doused the sack in coal oil.

"That's good," Lacey said to him. "Get on Sitting Bull and I'll ignite it."

Slocum swung into the saddle and tore out with his flaming trailer to the west, swung around to go east, and the grass behind caught on fire. Then he rode some south and drew another fire line across the land to burn up to his first one.

The crew beat out the first lane before it grew big enough to flare, and the fire was spreading south. The smoke was getting worse off the main fire, so Slocum drew his kerchief up over his nose and kicked Bull in the sides to keep him running. At last, satisfied with his progress, he tossed the rope and raced for the camp. The fire line was going to work. They'd have to fight any flames that licked past it, but they could control it from there on around their wagons.

Off his horse, he drank a dipper of water, joined by Lacey and Snow.

"Whew, without this, our efforts would never've been enough," Lacey said. "It would have overrun us and burned the wagons to the ground."

Slocum agreed. "We've got it done. Thank everyone."

Smoke coming off the wildfire was soon bad in camp. Everyone was coughing. He hugged Snow to his side. "We're tough firefighters, huh?"

"Yes, such a fire burned up a dozen of our tepees once up on the Big Horns. We never thought to start a fire to stop one. Squaws were so afraid they got on horses and rode away. My father was so mad when he and the hunters returned."

"I would have been mad, too. But this wasn't my first prairie fire either to outrun or fight."

Close to dark, the men and the horses and mules returned. They were surprised the camp hadn't burned, and also relieved.

Slocum's lead driver said, "We drove the horses across the river and I kept saying, 'That damn fire probably burned our rigs up.' Glad you all fought it."

"It damn sure wasn't easy," one of the men said, and they all laughed.

Jasper and Snow had supper ready. The big man announced, "Smoked buffalo."

More laughing.

After the meal, the two of them went to Slocum's wagon. Once they were inside, he hugged her tight, noting that they both stunk like the dead fire. But he didn't care. They'd saved the wagons for another day. He planned to soon head east. With luck, in another month they'd be back in Omaha. The shortage of feed for his stock on this next leg of the journey worried him more than anything.

He lifted the dress off over her head and outstretched arms. There, in the darkness, his precious present for the evening stood unwrapped. Having her along would sure make the days shorter.

Morning was cracking the horizon with rosy sunlight even before the fiery ball rose over the land. Headed east toward home, they passed the empty fort parade ground in a cloud of dust raised by iron rims and hooves. Slocum sat his stout horse, and Snow rode a bay at the head of the convoy. Johnson had gone ahead earlier to look for a place to stop midday to let the animals graze that afternoon.

His goal was to make twenty miles a day. Whether his goal would be met or not depended on being able to find a suitable source of forage for the stock each day.

Even this early in the day, clouds were moving in. It might rain somewhere over in Nebraska. They still had some miles to go in Wyoming before reaching that line. But the farther east they went, the greater the chance of rain. That could be good or bad. Enough to stimulate grass growing was ideal. Too much, and mud would be an anchor to slow them down. What the hell did he care? He had supplies enough to get back and Snow to share his bed.

Riding his crop-eared horse in a jog in her company, he could smile all day in relief. *Living high on the hog,* his pappy would have said.

8

They reached the Nebraska line the third day and waited for a long herd of longhorn cattle to pass by, headed north. The man who owned them, Jim Duggan of Kerrville, Texas, wore a trail-dusted business suit and a wide-brimmed hat. He stopped to talk to Slocum. Duggan tipped his hat to Snow and smiled.

"She makes pretty scenery up here. Where you been?"

"Billings, Montana."

"That's a fur piece."

"Where you heading?"

"A ranch in South Dakota. I knew it would be a helluva long haul, but I've been on this drive since March. They stole my remuda once. Of course, the Kansas authority turned me around and sent me back south—tick fever, they said. I rounded the curve to go up to Ogallala, and that trail was choked with cattle and no feed, so I went west. Drier out there, but we made it here."

"Sounds tough enough. We fought Indians on the Bozeman, and prairie fires."

"Ain't no easy turn in this business out here. I left a new woman expecting our first child. She's got family there. But I can't help her. I was planning to be back home to help her, and here I am two months from her delivery time, and then two months out from being home as well."

"Good luck to you, partner."

"Nice to meet you, Slocum. You too, missy." He rode on, the herd finally passed, and they went on as well.

So far, Johnson had found them enough grass every evening to sustain the animals. If they couldn't find grass as they moved on, Slocum planned to buy grain.

"Can we stop in Ogallala?" Lacey asked him.

"If we can rent or find pasture enough to catch the animals up."

"Let's send Johnson ahead to find it. We all need some rest and a little fun."

"Sure. Whethers or Indian Joe can also be the grass scout."

"Maybe send all of them. Johnson has done a super job so far."

Slocum agreed.

Plans were made that evening in camp. The scouts redeployed, and Jasper was to get a list of needed supplies to be ordered and ready for Slocum before they got to town. The rest of the men smiled at word of a layover.

Some squaw showed up after dark and quietly sold her ass to as many men as had money. She got a quarter a trip, which was highway robbery—most of them only charged a dime. She left, limping her away across the prairie before dawn with her leather purse full. In the predawn light, Slocum watched a buck come to meet her and bring a horse for her to belly up on. They rode off as prosperous Indians, and Slocum chuckled.

The scouts were back in forty-eight hours. Johnson had leased enough grass for the teams and a place to camp with a windmill to pump fresh water for ten bucks a day. Slocum thanked him. Two or three days wouldn't kill them. Now, if all his men made it back to camp still fit, he'd enjoy his part of the deal.

If things progressed as they had so far, he might make the goal he'd set to beat the winter. Three days later, they parked, set up camp, and he let half the crew go into town to raise billy-hell. The forage there would strengthen his animals. The fenced-in grass was super, and the well water a little slack tasting but it was much better than mud.

The last mile marker said OMAHA—THREE HUNDRED FIFTY MILES. When they'd gone in through the fenced pasture gate, he knew they'd make it before any serious weather erupted.

"You look pleased," she said after he dismounted beside her.

"A couple of days to catch up and we'll be back there before the snow flies."

She looked around to be certain they were enough alone. "Catch up on what?"

He whispered in her ear. "You, too."

She made a smug face. "That is good, too. I will smile."

"We both will smile."

With wagons parked and stock unharnessed, half the crew were on their way to spirits and angels—rotgut whiskey and whores. There'd probably be a few fights, but Slocum hoped none would be serious.

They'd all be ready to push on to Omaha after this layover and then burn that city down—but by then he wouldn't care what they did. After the breakdown of unharnessing and turning the stock loose where Johnson said it was well fenced, Slocum and Snow retired to the wagon and undressed. With her sprawled under him on the cot, he was about to partake of her sweet body when someone shouted his name.

"Slocum! You ole sumbitch, get out here. I heard you was coming and I aim to clean your damn plow. Right now, get out here."

"Who is that?" After he moved off her, she bolted up.

"Sam Clover, an old buddy of mine." He shook his head as she began to dress. "I'm coming. Don't burn the damn wagon. It ain't mine," he yelled.

She frowned at him. "He sounds funny."

"Snow, he ain't funny. He's crazy."

"Whatever." She straightened her dress on her hips.

"Don't you plan no big surprise party for me. I just got sober from the last one," Clover yelled.

Slocum stuck his head out. "We're coming, gawdamn you."

"Hell, I didn't know I was breaking up any baby making. Go ahead, I'll just sit out here and drink this good bottle of hooch I brought to celebrate your homecoming with."

Dressed, Slocum climbed out carrying his socks and boots. "Who told you I was coming here?"

"Aw, hell, everyone knew you were coming. Even them gawdamn snoopy agents from the Hawk Detective Agency knew you would be here."

"What the hell do they want of me?"

"A bank robbery in Kansas."

"Hell, when was that?"

"Month ago. Said you and your gang held up Abilene Bank and Trust."

"Aw, hell, Sam, I was in Billings, Montana, a month ago and can prove it."

"I got the newspaper report right here." He handed the folded paper to him. "I wondered when you turned bank robber. I knew we'd cross paths and I'd get to jab you about it—well, let a bumble bee sting my old pecker. Why, she is cuter than a field of Texas bluebonnets in the spring. Who's she?"

"Snow, the daughter of Man of Pipes."

"Ah, hell, them Cheyenne can get in the sack with a squaw and make the prettiest women on this earth, can't they?"

"She ain't yours, and I'm not going to share her with you."

"Since you robbed that bank in Kansas, you're getting not only stingy, but inhospitable."

"I was in Montana when this happened." He began to read the newspaper Sam had handed him.

> The First Bank and Trust was robbed yesterday just past noon. The gang leader was identified as John Slocum, a famous outlaw who with his gang of ten hardcore bad men stormed into the bank lobby. The men shoved around respectable ladies who were in the bank at the time. Their requests were so disgusting we can't repeat them on the pages of this family newspaper, but you can imagine them in your worst moments.
>
> Slocum, a longtime wanted criminal for dire deeds done elsewhere, swaggered around the bank and busted Billy Ushery, the cashier, over the head when he tried to stop him from sacking up all the gold, silver, and currency in his cashbox. After the outlaws rode out of our town, throwing hot lead at the innocent citizens in their way, Billy's injury required five stitches by Doctor Blaine.

Sheriff Tom Kane sent a telegram to the U.S. Marshal's office reporting the horrific incident and gave a list of the other known killers riding with Slocum. A posse was to be formed to chase down the criminals, but since these felons were so tough and well-armed, Sheriff Kane decided to leave their capture to federal officials, who are on their way here.

Bank President Aaron Hollis also wired the Hawk Detective Agency in Denver, Colorado, to pursue these bandits. We are awaiting word from that office on their plans to apprehend the gang.

In another note, the wife of rancher and businessman Edward Stokes has disappeared. Diane Stokes, age twenty-five, was reported missing an hour after the robbery. It is suspected that when the gang left on their escape route, they may have stopped at the Stokes ranch house for supplies and food, and then kidnapped her. No sign of the lady has shown up. According to her husband, Michael, his wife was of sound mind and never would have left her fine home unless taken as a hostage. He is offering a thousand dollars for her safe return. Mrs. Stokes is twenty-five years old, five feet nine inches tall, weighs 130 pounds, and has light brown hair and blue eyes. Anyone who knows her whereabouts can report it to the Stokes Mercantile or Sheriff Kane.

"Who in the hell is this gang, anyway?"

"The Slocum Gang, is all I know."

"Sam, I was in Billings a month ago. Who do you think set me up?"

"Can you imagine ten men, plus the leader, in that small bank lobby? Why, they must have been falling over each other propositioning those fancy women in there to fuck them."

"I can't even imagine an eleven-member gang pulling off a robbery."

"Well, the storekeeper's wife ain't showed up yet either. Where did you stash her?" Sam laughed.

"I bet she simply rode off with them."

"I don't know him, but I figure that was the case, too."

"How did you know I was coming?"

"I met Buster Johnson when he came to rent this pasture. He told me you ramrodded this outfit, so I came to warn you."

"Crap, I don't have time to be hauled down to Kansas to prove I was in Montana when the robbery was committed."

"That's what I figured. You better pack a bag and shag ass out of here."

"It won't take them long to know I'm out here. I better go talk to Lacey and tell him he's going to have to get this outfit back to Omaha."

"Where does she need to go?" He gave a head toss at Snow.

"Fort Robinson. They're holding her people up there until next spring. Then they'll march them down to Fort Reno and the new agency there in the Indian Territory."

"Oh boy, that will be a real nice trip."

"I can't help that."

"I know that. How can I help you?" asked Sam.

"I imagine you have your own problems, but I appreciate the offer." He turned to Snow. "Go find Lacey. We need to make new plans."

She nodded and took off to find his man. In a short while, she returned with him.

"This is Sam Clover. He brought news that I'm being sought for a Kansas bank robbery, that happened while we were in Montana. I don't need to let them arrest me, take me there, and then have to prove I was in Billings."

"That makes sense. You want me to take the train on?"

"Yes, I do. I'll contact them in Omaha and tell them where to send my share. I have records for my expenses, and there's money left to buy supplies to easily get you back."

"I'll do my best. Hope I don't have another prairie fire to fight."

"It may be the search for grass to feed the stock that vexes you the most. I'll be on my way in a half hour."

"Damn nice to work with you. Snow, Jasper will cry when he learns you're gone."

"I'll meet you north of the Platte River Bridge in an hour," Sam said. "I'll ride along, in case you get into any trouble."

"That might work. Snow, do we need a packhorse?"

"Yes."

"I'll get them saddled and bring them over here," Lacey said.

Slocum agreed and said to her. "Make us two bedrolls, too."

She nodded and climbed back in the end of his wagon to get some of their things together.

Slocum shook Sam's hand before Sam left to get his own things, in order to meet them north of the bridge as planned.

When Lacey brought the horses, Slocum already had the saddles out and ready.

His man had read the newspaper Sam brought. "You're right. We were in Montana when that bank was robbed. Who said it was you?" he asked.

"He must have announced my name when he told them to hold up their hands."

"Crazy world. But we turned a tough deal into a working arrangement. I'm proud I worked with you. And all of us love Snow."

Lacey hugged her. "We hope you're reunited with your tribe, and happy."

"I will do what I must for my people."

"Sure, but we'll miss both of you."

They wound up the loading, and Slocum shook Lacey's hand. "I took two hundred dollars from this purse. I marked it down. They owe me more than that. Tell the rest of the men I'm sorry I missed telling them."

He boosted Snow onto her horse and then swung up on Bull. The men nearby, knowing Slocum was leaving, wished him well. He waved to them. Snow took the packhorse lead, and they rode out of camp for the gate. No need to hesitate. They had to be gone before some snoopy detectives came around.

One thing Slocum knew for sure, they needed to slip across the Platte River Bridge. From rains upstream, the river was too high to swim across, so he sent Snow ahead, and he melted in among some ranch cowboys and a chuck wagon.

Across the river at last, he hoped unobserved, he short loped to catch Snow, and they eventually met up with Sam. On the road to Fort Robinson, they held their horses in a hard trot and made good progress north.

"How far away is it?" Slocum asked

"Two hundred miles," Sam said, looking over his shoulder for any pursuit.

"We can make it there in a week or less."

"I bet so. But our asses will pay the price." Sam laughed. "I don't see any dust back there, so we must have a good lead on them."

They found a small store in late afternoon and bought some oats for their horses. The man's wife offered to feed them supper for fifty cents. Slocum agreed, and they ate the meal in the couple's living quarters. The food was favorable, and her coffee and apple pie delicious. They camped nearby on the prairie and left before dawn.

Slocum wanted to get Snow to her people, then they could take it from there. He felt grateful to have Sam along. An extra set of eyes always helped in an escape situation. He'd be glad to have her safely there. *Damn, he'd sure miss her sweet body and company.*

9

The road to Fort Robinson covered lots of rolling prairie.
There were still remnants scattered around of the once huge
buffalo herds that roamed all the West. Here and there, on
a watercourse, a brave soul had established a farm or ranch.
They stopped for the night at a Texan's ranch. The rancher
had built a huge sod house and barn to house his crew of
cowboys, with their horses in one end to prevent thefts by
renegade Indians.

Bill Borne had a half-black wife, Nelly, who stood six
feet tall and towered over most of his dozen ranch hands
they met later. A warm, friendly woman with several of her
young offspring around her dress, she met them in the windswept yard.

"Get down. My man will be here shortly. He'll love to
talk to you and learn what's happening in the world out
there."

Bill Borne was equally a giant of a man, with huge hands
to shake and a drawl to his words. "We don't get many folks

to stop by here. Glad she got you to stop. Me and the boys get tired of our own company. The two thousand cattle we brought up here are doing good. But, hell, where else would they get this much grass in the world?

"Most of the Injuns are friendly, and we've raised plenty of potatoes and things for us to eat. But, like always, there's some sour apples that steal horses rather than break mustangs. Plenty of good horses out here. We had to break several to replace the ones they stole. But we got them put up now, inside the back of our house, and enough hay inside to feed them for winter."

"You brought cows," Slocum said.

"Most of them are cows. I bought some Durham bulls to cross them and get some hair on my future cattle for winter, plus the crosses bring more money for beef."

"How long have you been here?" Slocum asked.

"Three years."

"Well, you look dug in here."

"I think we are."

Slocum told them about their plans to return Snow to her tribe, and where he had been through the summer. By the time he wound it up, Borne said, "She's got food ready. We better go eat. She won't run out, but those hands of mine eat everything loose."

He laughed and herded them into the dining area, where he showed them seats.

"These folks are going to Fort Robinson. This young lady's tribe is being held up there for moving to the Indian Territory," he told his crew.

The crew nodded and told them, "Hello."

One of the young ones rose and said, "No disrespect intended, but I'd keep her here and save you all the trip."

His words drew laughter.

After the meal, they talked. Snow and Nelly visited on

the side, and when they turned in, Snow told Slocum, "She is a powerful woman. He came up here to escape the prejudice of a white man's and a black woman's marriage in Texas. She misses her people, like I miss mine."

Slocum nodded that he understood. They slept separately in the large room Borne had offered them and were up before dawn. Nelly had a big spread for breakfast. She spoke of the many hawks that threatened her poultry population. Her shotgun was kept loaded and handy, so she thought she was depleting their population. She'd fried some of her chicken's eggs for her company.

They rode off in their slickers, under a thick cloud cover all morning and the threat of rain coming. It began with thunder and they sought shelter.

A deserted sod house half-fallen-in made a good place to stop. They used a room for their horses and found enough wood to build a fire, and the smoke escaped out the missing roof section.

"You find these places abandoned and wonder about the story behind them," Sam said. "Where I was raised west of Fort Worth, the Comanches raided places in that area every fall. When I was four, my mother hid me when she heard them coming. They killed her, and neighbors found me wandering around the place calling for her. I didn't know she couldn't hear me."

"Did your father take another wife?" Snow asked.

"He did, and she had kids. They'd killed her husband in another raid. Even though I was so young, it never was the same. I kept thinking my real mother would come back and take me away to a better place than the crowded one we had."

"When did you realize she wasn't coming back?" Snow asked.

"About when I turned twelve. I knew she was dead and never coming home, so I ran away."

"Did they try to return you?"

"No, I was one less mouth they'd have to feed. That woman had a baby every nine months. My paw must have turned more fertile. I was their only child, then here came this gal who was a baby factory. I never looked back. I was hungry lots of times, but good folks helped me. I soon was working ranches where you did things from horseback, and I never picked another boll of that gawdamn cotton."

They laughed.

"I hate cotton so bad."

"How does it grow?" Snow asked.

Sam said, "It is a stickery little plant you have to bend over to pick the bolls and cotton from and put them in a sack you drag between your legs down the row."

"It only grows in the South," Slocum said.

"Thank God," Sam said with a shake of his head.

"Did you ever go back to see them?"

Sam shook his head. "When I left, I left for good. My real ma was my savior, and she was dead and her grave unmarked."

Slocum nodded that he understood, as thunder rolled across the sky and more rain fell.

"How far are we from the fort?" Snow asked.

"We should be there in a week,"

The next day the sky cleared, and they reached a small settlement at midday. Kerry's Corner—a store, two saloons, a blacksmith, and corrals. A few sod houses and some tents housed the people. The structures were all slapdash thrown-up. The raw cut lumber was mixed with salvaged wood from another time and place.

The three of them went in the Culpepper Saloon and ordered supper. Sam and Slocum each had a beer, and Snow had coffee. The bartender, Oscar, was polite and conversational.

"She's pretty."

"Yes, a real attractive Indian girl," Slocum said.

"Not many of them are that pretty."

Slocum was nodding in agreement when several horses arrived in the street and a rowdy bunch came in the saloon led by a big man in buckskin who needed a barber. The hard bunch of whites and breeds in frontier dress lined up at the bar, and the big man bought several bottles and ordered glasses for them.

His men settled in, downing it, and he hooked his elbows on the bar and gazed at the three of them.

"My name's Abraham Grosbeck."

"Slocum's mine," he said and nodded at Sam. "Sam Clover, and her name is Snow." He took a bite of his dinner.

"An interesting-looking squaw. What would you take for her?"

"She ain't for sale."

"No, I mean how much money do you want for her?"

Slocum laid down his fork. "Mister, she ain't for sale at no price. She is not mine to sell, so go on dreaming. You're not getting her."

"I have twelve men here to back me."

"And we may not get them all, but I can guarantee you will die in the damn shoot-out."

Sam's chair scooted aside to face them. The men turned slowly and frowned at what was about to explode.

"You boys drink your whiskey. I can handle this matter," Grosbeck said with authority.

"You're a smart man," Sam said and took another bite of food.

"You two must have figured out: What I want I get. Now, I've got money enough to buy her ass."

Slocum eyed him and then took another bite of his supper. "No, you don't. She ain't for sale. Period. Don't mention it again. Bartender, bring me my bill. I'm leaving this place—with her, too."

"Señor, there is no bill."

"Fine. I'll leave the money on this table." He motioned for Snow to get up. "We'll be leaving. Any man sticks his head out the door after us will die. Good evening."

"Let's settle this. Sorry you took offense at my words. But trust me, what I want I get."

"Grosbeck, even God don't get all he wants in this world, so stay out of my way."

"You can talk tough now, but the next time it will be different."

"Yes, you'll be dead."

"I'll have to see that."

"You won't after I close your eyelids."

The money on the table, Slocum read the fear written on the bartender's face. Sam pushed Snow ahead toward the batwing doors. Slocum surveyed the men, his sweaty fist on his gun grips, ready for any move.

Outside, Sam and Snow mounted and had the packhorse before Slocum let the doors fly back. While Slocum mounted, Sam took a shot at the door frame. His bullet splintered wood in the face of a gunman, who screamed and fell backward. His gun discharged into the ceiling.

The three whipped their horses and fled the community. Slocum cast a last look back. They had no pursuit—so far. But, like a venomous snake, Slocum knew Grosbeck would seek revenge. He and his men were the kind that didn't take such affronts and forget them.

From there on, they had to sleep light and guarded. But Slocum would push to get Snow safe with her own people, and if he had to kill Grosbeck and his entire army, he would have no grief. He knew, however, that his enemy was powerful enough and mean enough to keep after him.

"Them sons-a-bitches need to go to the Indian burial grounds feet-first," Sam said, checking the loads in his handgun.

"We ain't heard the last of them, and that worries me more than anything else."

"So true. So true, brother. And we need to cut them down in numbers. If we get the chance."

"I think we'll get the chance. If they ever jump us, run like hell," Slocum said to Snow.

She only nodded.

"What do we have left?" Sam asked.

"Oh, maybe a hundred miles."

"Well, we better have eyes in the back of our heads."

"It could be tough."

They camped well off the road that evening. They took turns on guard, and Sam woke Slocum before dawn. Snow, too.

"They're all around us," he whispered. "I've got both my guns ready. They're coming in on all sides."

Slocum nodded, and told Snow to get under the covers. He had on his boots and saw that they had some cover around them from box elder bushes. Then, suddenly, there was a charge by Grosbeck's gang members, and the camp came alive with armed men, some with ax handles. Sam brought down a few with his pistol, and Slocum took out four of them before having his head pounded in and going unconscious.

Slocum came to hours later. A headache blasted his brain. Not ten feet away, Sam lay dead, sightless eyes staring at the sky. No sign of Snow—they must have taken her. As he climbed to his feet, he wondered how much was broken in his body. Sam needed to be buried. All the horse stock was gone. They'd taken the supplies and packhorse, too. Hell, they had got everything but the hair on his head.

No shovel, but he found a Bowie knife and set in to carve Sam a grave. It was slow, and he was still digging when the moon rose. Some buffalo wolves came slinking around. He saw them and wished he had a fire, but he had no fuel and no time to gather it.

"Get out!" he screamed. No gun to shoot at them, he went on digging. His fingers were raw and hurt him, but everything else did, too. Close to dawn, he buried Sam and hoped the grave was deep enough to keep the damn wolves from digging his corpse up. He found some crackers and jerky in a discarded saddlebag. God only knew how old they were. At the small creek nearby, he drank water and set out to find help. On the road, a man stopped and asked who'd tried to kill him.

"You seen any gang with a squaw?"

"No."

"Are you going south?"

"Yes. I have business in Ogallala."

"I need to bum a ride down to a ranch belongs to Bill Borne. He might stake me to a horse, gun, and money."

"He's the Texan has a black wife, isn't that him?"

"Yes, she's a nice lady."

"A white man married a black woman in Texas, and he had to leave the state, didn't he?"

"I don't think many folks would mess with him."

"Aw, he'd have to defend her over and over again. What did they take from you?"

"My money, guns, my horses, my good friend Sam, and the Cheyenne princess I was taking back to her people."

"Must be tough bastards. You need to stop and see a doctor."

"No. I need to get to Borne's place."

"Take us all today and tomorrow to get down there."

"You can stand me, I can stand the trip."

"You damn sure look tough."

"Don't worry about me."

Slocum near passed out several times, and only by sheer grit and little sleep did he finally arrive at the ranch. Nelly's voice, and those of the men, sounded serious, like he looked near death. As hard as he tried, he found no voice of his own.

Nelly's long white-sided fingers flashed in his face. "You're near dead, Slocum. Don't waste no words on us. We be going to get you better. Lots better."

He closed his eyes in relief—he had reached his goal.

10

His vision wavered as he looked up at Nelly's dark face while lying in the stranger's wagon bed. "Hi, lady. I don't mean to burden you, but I need some help. They got Snow and killed my buddy Sam."

"Land's sakes, Slocum, they damn near got you, from what I sees."

"I need to go look for them."

"I'm going to have to patch you up first. Bill, he be back and will know what to do. Meanwhile, I be giving you a big dose of laudanum and you get some rest. Now, mister, you helps me get him in de bed."

"I told him he needed to see a doctor, but he wouldn't listen," his rescuer said.

"I's know all about stubborn men. I gots me one of dem, too."

Strong arms lifted Slocum from the wagon. The man had his arms, Nelly had his legs, and they took him into the house, where she put him in the bed in the living room. Last thing he recalled was when she gave him a big dose of medicine and he fell sound asleep.

The big, booming voice of Borne woke him. "You coming around?"

His own weak voice shocked him. "I'm trying."

"Now, I've heard stories. Tell me what happened to you."

"I ran into an army of thugs up at Kerry's Corner, led by Abraham Grosbeck. He wanted to buy Snow. I told him to go to hell. That night they overran my camp, killed Sam Clover, took Snow, and left me for dead. That was a couple of days ago. I need to find her."

"You need to heal some. You're in tough shape. That damn Grosbeck needs putting away, but in your shape you'd be killed on sight."

"I need to get her out of his clutches."

"You may do that in top shape. Not like you are right now. Rest a few weeks. I'll find out where he's at, then you can go get him."

"He will have hurt her by then."

"Damnit, Slocum, let Nelly get you strong enough. I have horses to ride, guns for you to shoot, but damned if I'm letting you out with them till you're stronger and can fight that gang. Otherwise, taking them on would be pure suicide for you."

"All right, Bill, but I'll hate every minute I ain't looking for her."

"You just will live that much longer. I have a half-breed Sioux boy I trust that can go look for them and keep track of them. He can come back in a week and report where they're staying. That way, when you get strong enough, you can ride right to them."

"Warn him that they're mean sons-a-bitches. They tricked Sam and me."

"Oh, he knows them well. Everyone up here hates them.

They gang rape squaws, as well as white women on isolated homesteads. They know they'd have to kill me to get to Nelly, but I don't take any chances."

"Thanks. I'm about to go out of my mind worrying about her."

"It won't be easy getting her back either."

"What does he do for money, besides rob people?"

"They hear of anyone with money on the Fort Robinson road, they rob and kill them, plus usually dispose of their bodies. They must have been on the run when they raided you. You're lucky."

"No luck about it. They went looking for us. Surrounded the camp and charged in with guns and ax handles. We got about four or five of them—shot or shot up."

"Then they're licking their wounds. How many men did he have in the saloon?"

"Twelve."

"Hell, you two whipped up on him. That was damn near half his force."

"I guess you're right. I never saw him there."

"Hell, he's like some damn colonel in the army; he ain't risking his hide getting skinned."

"I bet you're right about that."

"I'll bring Noko by in the morning when the boys are gone. We can talk to him then about finding the gang. Get some rest and heal."

"Thanks, Bill. I appreciate both of you."

"No problem. Get some sleep."

Nelly fed him another tablespoon of laudanum and smiled. "You are one tough guy, Slocum. They ever ask me about Texas men, I tell 'em I knew two, Bill and yous." Then she left, laughing aloud.

He went to sleep, concerned about Snow's welfare in Grosbeck's clutches . . .

11

The next morning, Bill brought Noko by and the Sioux youth squatted on his boot heels close by on the floor.

"You know Grosbeck and his gang," Bill said to the boy of maybe eighteen.

"If they catch you sneaking around, they'll kill you," Slocum warned.

The youth nodded. "They won't catch me. Those breeds are not half-Sioux."

"One thing, if you can get the woman out with you and get her away without harm, I'll pay you well."

"I will watch close, if I can. No harm, I understand that, too."

"He's all fixed up to go. I told him to check back in a week to tell us where they are."

"Noko," Slocum said. "Be careful. They're all killers."

"I understand. They won't get me."

Bill walked him out to his horse. Slocum sat up and used crutches to go outside and relieve himself. He'd need to do lots more healing to ever ride a horse ten miles. Swinging on his homemade crutches, he went back to bed.

Noko didn't return on Monday, the appointed day he was to come back. Slocum was anxious until late Tuesday, when a haggard youth rode in on a jaded horse. When he dismounted and made a beeline to Bill and Slocum on the porch, he took some razzing from the crew.

"Sons-a-bitches are up by Fort Robinson. The girl is okay. They watch her like a hawk. Once, I thought I'd get her out, but they had her covered too good."

"What are they doing up there?" Slocum asked.

"Trying to sell cattle to the agency is what I learned."

"They don't have any cattle. Whose cattle would they sell?" Bill asked.

"Maybe yours, huh? They talk about selling them three hundred head," said Noko.

"Those bastards ain't stealing my cattle."

Noko shrugged. "Homesteaders don't have that many, if you stole from all of them."

"You're right as rain about that."

"How long will they be up there?" Slocum asked.

"I don't know. Depends if they get the contract. Four of them are wounded. They got them in camp. I think you killed one more."

"Then he only has a handful of men left, huh?" Bill asked.

The boy nodded.

Nelly came and took the weary youth into the kitchen to eat and then to get some sleep.

Slocum wondered if he could ride clear up there and then fight them. Maybe in another week he could, but hell would only know where they'd be by then.

"When Noko's rested, he can go out and scout for them again," Bill said. "You get some more sleep. You must be mending, since you're only using one crutch."

Slocum made a face in disgust. In another week, he was packing up and going after them—if he had to walk.

Noko slept for twenty-four hours, then Bill sent him with supplies and a fresh horse back to scouting Grosbeck and his gang until the next week.

That week, Slocum split Nell lots of stove wood. His strength was coming back, and he hoped he'd be strong enough soon to ride all day. He'd eventually find them and get Snow out of their camp.

Bill telegraphed Omaha for him, and later that week, the cowboy who went for their mail brought a package for Slocum from his former employers. It contained four hundred dollars, and they still owed him two hundred more. Since they knew he moved a lot, they'd hold it until he wired them again.

After a big argument, Bill sold him a stout bay horse and saddle, a packhorse and pack saddle, a good bedroll, some utensils, and enough supplies for a few weeks. That included a used .45 Colt and holster and a Winchester rifle, all with ammo. They settled on one-seventy. Bill wanted him to simply take it all for nothing, but in the end he took the money.

Noko returned. The army, for some reason, didn't buy the beef from Grosbeck—some Dakota beef contractor made the deal. The outlaw and his men were denned up in some canyon. The boy thought the gang might winter there in some abandoned cabins. They had hay for the horses piled up. The canyon had three ways out, too. He had seen Snow but wasn't able to get her out of their hands.

The boy was going to sleep for a day, and then he'd take Slocum back up there. Slocum almost didn't sleep that night, he was so antsy about getting Snow away from them.

They left the ranch the following morning. Nelly hugged and kissed Slocum good-bye, and Bill and the cowboys all shook his hand and wished him good luck. Bill even offered to go along, but Slocum convinced him he needed to stay there. Between the renegade Sioux war parties and the other outlaws roaming the land, he needed to worry about his own place and wife. Parting was almost sad, since he knew he could never repay them for the care and concern they'd given him during his recovery.

At their parting, Bill brushed his words of thanks aside. "Leave that damn Grosbeck for the magpies to eat. That will be payment enough for me."

Jogging the bay horse north on the Fort Robinson road, Slocum had that intention in mind. *Leave him for dead . . .*

12

The two pushed hard for the fort. Noko had some kinfolks there keeping track of the outlaws for him. Without the summer heat, the days were pleasant, and a jumper felt good until mid-morning each day. There was freight traffic on the road, folks heading back before the snow flew. A few outfits were hauling goods up there for both the army and the Red Cloud Agency. They might not get back to Omaha before it snowed, but winter might hold off. It was always a fickle bitch that time of year.

They camped with Noko's relatives. One of his cousins, a tall woman in her early twenties named Blue Swan, came by when dark came. A widow, she told Slocum, as she led him away from the campfire.

"Noko said he would take care of the horses and I could entertain you tonight. If you would like me to?"

"Why, I'd love for you to. Where will we go?"

"Let's use my lodge."

He agreed.

She looked around, then wrapped tight in her blanket, she led him through the row of tepees. He entered her tepee on his hands and knees. In the darkness, he sat down on his butt. At her fire ring she squatted, shed her blanket, and soon had a small fire going, her dark face reflected the flames.

"You are a big man," she said. "My man was killed at the fight with Crook at Rosebud. I have not slept with any man since then, but you reminded me so much of him, I thought he had came back or maybe his spirit had. Do you have a wife?"

"No."

"Good. Then I am not stealing you from her."

He nodded and laughed softly. "No, you are not stealing me from anyone."

"Good. Take your clothes off. Noko won't miss you. He has a cousin who loves him when he comes back here."

"A cousin?"

"Oh, yes, they once planned to be married, but his mother had a fit. His girlfriend is a double cousin. Their parents were brother and sister. His mother said it was bad luck for them to marry—so they sleep together when they get the chance. It is a shame. But these are the ways of my people, the Sioux, I guess."

"All people have some such things that make little sense when you are in love."

"Oh, yes." She was in the process of shedding her buckskin dress off over her head.

Undressed, she crawled under the blanket on her pallet. He wrapped the holster around his pistol and put it close to the bed, then completed getting undressed.

He joined her, and in the dim light, he saw her smile.

"Tell me about the mean men you are after."

"They killed my friend, Sam, for little money. Beat me up badly. I think they thought I'd die, too. They took a woman, a Cheyenne, who I was taking back to her people at Red Cloud's agency. We'll find and kill the men who have her and take her on up there. What do you wish from me tonight, if I have the power to give it to you?"

"I would like to leave this world with you. It is a sad one for me, and I want you to take me places far away, so spare nothing. I am yours."

"I will try my damnedest."

She wrapped her arms around him. He reached in and lifted her chin to kiss her on the mouth. Even in the tepee's darkness, he saw her eyes fly open in shock. No one had ever kissed her before—she would be easy to bring to a boil.

She was thin-bodied for an Indian woman, but her breasts were still proud, and she quickly began to moan when he teased her womanhood with his finger. They soon were connected. She felt tight-fitting at his entry, and many muscles ran the depth of her vagina. Oh, damn, what a woman. Free as the wind, she gave herself entirely to him. Many neat white women acted free, but they held back a reserve—like, *You can't have all of my body and definitely not all the control of it.*

Swan gave him one hundred percent, and the power of that made him stronger and more powerful than he ever could have been with a less receptive woman. They went flying away to where the stars shone and produced brilliance to their bond, made him close his eyes and grind at loving her. Their efforts were like a great magnetic force that drew them to each other. Their pubic bones rubbed hard on the coarse hairs that kept them from being totally one body. Greater than wonderful. Better than most. Hotter than a blacksmith's fire. And then he came. She fainted, limp in his grasp.

"Oh, my God. You are the most powerful man I have ever known. Stay with me. I could face the sunrises and not be saddened by him being gone anymore. Or wish he was here to love me at night—I would have you."

"Let's sleep. I'm still recovering from that beating two weeks ago. But you are a wonderful woman, and in the night, if you need me, wake me and I'll do it again."

"I want to 'kiss' you, like you did me."

"Kiss away."

She'd soon learn how. He hugged her tight, closed his eyes, and fell asleep.

Sometime in the night, they shared another such experience, and he dropped asleep again holding her naked form tight to him. What a delightful repast with a woman that deserved a real man to love her. Someday she would find one, and he hoped her new one appreciated her skills as much as he did.

Noko had the horses saddled and ready to go at dawn. Swan apologized for not making Slocum breakfast, but he dismissed her concern, kissed her, and rode off, gnawing on dry jerky and recalling his night of pleasure.

"This woman you were with last night, Swan said you are prohibited from marrying her?"

Noko bobbed his head. Slocum chewed on the smoky-flavored dry meat. Obviously, his companion was not talking about his situation. They reached the top of the windswept grassy hill, and he reined to a stop in the soft morning breeze.

"When this is over, I have decided I will marry her regardless of who tells me things. She and I have been lovers since we were children. She doesn't want anyone else. I don't want anyone else. Why we have no offsprings, we do not know. We have tried to make a baby, so we could say that is why we wish to marry, but the spirits have avoided us. Nothing can stand in our way. When you are through with me, I will marry her."

"You can go back now and marry her."

He shook his head and booted his horse off the top. "No, I promised Bill to help you. My word is my word."

"I wish you and her many happy years."

Noko nodded and rode on. He turned back and said, "Swan is a good woman. When she gets over grieving, I hope she finds a man."

"Oh, she will."

"Good. I know the old days are gone, but I liked them much better."

"Yes, the old days, when we were innocent, were much better than today with all our troubles and trials. A man gave them my name when he held up a bank in Kansas."

"So the law looks for you?"

Slocum nodded.

"That is worse than what happened to me. What will you do when this is over?"

"Fade away for a while. I've done it before."

"How will they know who you are?"

Slocum laughed and pushed up beside him. "Hopefully, they won't."

The outlaws had set up camp in a deep canyon covered in a forest of lodgepole pines. These patches of hills rose out of the grassy portion of northwest Nebraska, close to Wyoming and South Dakota. Their own horses hobbled two miles away, they climbed over a rugged mountain, then through his brass telescope Slocum studied the several low-walled cabins and the cooking smoke. He thought he saw Snow once, but there were several Indian women in the camp working on butchering deer and fleshing hides. He counted four different ones.

The best thing he found was Sitting Bull among their horses. He'd missed the crop-eared buffalo chaser.

He also saw bandaged members of the gang, walking

around with an arm in a sling or on crutches. He counted four of them that would not be great fighters, if he and Noko tried to take the camp. But there was no sight of the main man, Abraham Grosbeck. He must have left someone in charge, but so far Slocum hadn't seen anyone who might lead this group.

"I haven't seen Grosbeck."

Noko, who also did some scoping while they sat on the mountainside, agreed. "He must be away."

"I think we can go down there at night, cut their throats quietly, and take the camp."

Noko nodded. "Maybe then they will be drunk, too."

"They're drinking hard right now."

"Yes. We can move closer. I only saw one man with a rifle."

Slocum agreed. "Just be careful. I don't want her hurt."

"I was down there once, and I almost took her away, but my horse was back where we left ours, and I knew they'd be in hot pursuit."

With a bob of his head, Slocum said, "You've done well. I wish I knew where Grosbeck was, but if we get her out of there, I'll be happy. I can get him anytime."

"At dark, we can take them on, right?"

"Yes. Do they have dogs?"

"Not the last time. I have not seen any today."

"Good. Quiet-like, we'll go down there and take them tonight."

They went back over the hill to rest until dark. The moon would rise late, so they would have cover.

"Maybe they will have some of that venison cooked for us when we get through."

Slocum laughed. "That would be nice."

"I am tired of jerky."

"Me, too. I bet those women can fix us something."

Hat over his face, the warm sun on him, Slocum slept some. When darkness came, they were on the hillside, concealed close by one of the cabins. They'd noticed one guard—a man with a rifle walking about. He looked like Grosbeck's only camp guard. With stealth, they moved into the camp. The gang's horses were in a pen, snoring and shuffling, with an occasional kick and fit at one another. Slocum spotted the rifle-bearing one sitting in a ladder-back chair on a small porch, with the Winchester across his lap and smoking a quirley in the starlight.

The rest of the camp was quiet. If not asleep, they'd gone to bed. Slocum slipped up on the guard, conked him over the head, then cut his throat. Noko grabbed the rifle, while Slocum dragged the guard by the armpits to the side of a cabin, out of sight.

A woman came out of one cabin to squat and pee. Before she stood up, Noko had her mouth covered and whispered in her ear as he made her rise. Slocum saw her nod her head as she agreed. His man drew her back in the shadows with them.

He watched carefully for any more activity. "Ask her where the Cheyenne woman is."

The woman pointed to a cabin and spoke in Sioux.

Noko said, "Says she is in chains."

"We can get her later. Where are the other men?"

"One is in her cabin."

Slocum nodded. "You want to kill him, or shall I?"

"I can kill him. Two others sleep in that cabin beside where she is being held."

"Where is Grosbeck? Ask her. There's three more somewhere. I counted four wounded and the armed guard."

Noko agreed and asked her in Sioux where the other three were.

"She says one rode off to get some whiskey."

"When will he be back?"

More Sioux dialect was exchanged. "She says tomorrow, and she does not know where Grosbeck went, but he took two men with him."

"Probably to rob a stagecoach. We need to be aware he might come back."

Noko agreed, set down the rifle, drew his big knife, and went in the cabin. He returned shortly and wiped his blade on his pants. "He won't rob no more."

Slocum thanked him, then he and Noko went for the last two outlaws. They slipped into the cabin, and the two snoring men were easy to locate. With his cocked pistol in a sleeping man's face, Slocum ordered him up and on his feet. Noko did the same to his man, and they took both of them outside dressed in their long johns and bare footed. They seated them on the ground with their hands tied behind them.

With all secure, Slocum went to Snow's cabin and kicked in the door. After he lit the lamp, he found Snow. She was huddled on the bed in irons, fearful it was one of his men busting in to rape her. Seated on the bed, he held her tight.

"It's going to be all right. We have the others that are in camp," he told her.

"I thought they had killed you." Snow sobbed into his chest.

"They didn't, but they beat me up pretty bad, and I had to rest at the Borne ranch to recover. That's Noko with me. Where are the keys?"

"On the wall, by the door."

Noko tossed the keys to him, and Slocum unlocked her hands. She rubbed her raw wrists while he undid her leg irons.

"Are you all right?" he asked.

"Now you are here, I am fine."

"I'm sorry, but when they got through with me, I couldn't even ride a horse."

"I thought you were dead. They killed poor Sam, didn't they?"

"I buried him. Where did Grosbeck go?"

"To rob a bank. He was afraid to take his gang, so there were two of them, and they went separate to not raise suspicion."

He hugged her tight.

"The women say they will feed us good," Noko said after Slocum introduced him to Snow.

"That sounds good."

"What will you do with those men outside?"

"Hang them for murdering Sam. Two are already dead. One of the women told us one man went for whiskey."

"I think his name is Waites. He is no good and mean," Snow said.

"We'll catch him, and he won't be mean for long."

"I almost took you away from here one day," Noko said to Snow. "But I told Slocum I feared we couldn't get to my horse fast enough."

"Was that about two weeks ago?"

"Yes."

"I felt your presence that day. But when you left, I felt my spirits had left me."

"It was the smart thing to do," Slocum said.

"Oh, I agree. But when I felt your presence, I just knew I would be free of them."

Noko nodded that he understood. "I think the other women are pleased, too. Come, the food will soon be fixed. I am so glad to meet you, Snow."

"The pleasure is mine. And my people are at the fort?"

"Yes," Slocum said. "They are prisoners though, so they don't run away."

"I would gladly have been a prisoner with them, than what existed here for me."

Slocum led her out into the night to take a seat beside the blazing fire the women had built. Two women who were talking like magpies to Noko soon joined the three who sat on the ground. Slocum guessed they talked about Snow's future at the Red Cloud Agency for the Sioux.

Slocum told the women they were safe and could go back to their people when all this was over. His words settled them down, and food soon came heaped on tin plates. There was lots of tender venison in rich gravy, new potatoes, wild turnips, chokecherries, and garlic onions in a stew. It tasted wonderful to Slocum's longtime jerky-eating taste buds. The coffee could have been stronger, but he never complained.

"Hey, mister, what about us?" one of the prisoners shouted.

"You two won't live long enough to need any food. Better get to praying. Come sunup, you'll meet your maker."

"You ain't the law, you can't hang us."

"We're the law in this land. You killed a good man and stole our horses. Both are death penalty cases, and you two are guilty. The sentence is, come daybreak, to hang both of you by the neck until dead."

There was no more talk from the rope-bound prisoners. Noko found Slocum the hemp to make nooses, and they decided the outlaws could both be hung on the crossbar over the corral gate. They tossed ropes over the crossbar and tied them off. Kicking and cussing, the two men were hoisted onto saddled horses.

At Slocum's direction, Noko stood on another saddled horse to adjust the nooses around their necks. Then, with them affixed properly, he got off and stood behind the prisoner's horse on the right, with Slocum behind the left one.

When he asked if they had anything to say, the Indian women yipped, the prisoners were silent, and he and Noko sent them to hell by shouting and beating on their horses' asses. The crossbar sagged under their weight, but both their necks snapped, and silence fell on the onlookers.

One of the women broke into a war dance and stomped around the still swinging bodies, whooping and chanting as she went. Then the other three joined in and did the same thing.

"Join them, if you like," he said to Snow.

"No. I will dance when I am with my own people."

"I will bring our horses down here. Will the one who went for whiskey come back here?" Noko asked Slocum.

"Not fast enough for me. Let's take these women back to Fort Robinson, and Snow to her people. They can share the horses left here and the items they want to take, and then we'll burn this place down so no outlaws can use it for their hideout again."

"I will go get our horses and things and be back. I'll tell them about your plans. They can go home very rich women, with their guns, iron kettles, tin plates, bedrolls, and the hides they have tanned."

"And we'll split the money found on the outlaws, and any they hid here."

After Noko told them, the women ran to the cabins, and soon there were many coins and paper money poured out on a blanket. Slocum rode in and cut down the dead outlaws. They were searched for money and money belts, and then their bodies were carried into one of the cabins Slocum planned to burn.

The money was divided in half. Slocum only wanted a hundred for his part and that left three-fifty for Noko. That meant each woman had a hundred and ten apiece. A fortune for an Indian woman. Two of the women made leather pouches for Noko's money. By the time he returned and learned of his good fortune, the pouches were finished.

"You should take more of this," Noko said. "I am just a helper."

"No, you're getting married. I'll just be moving on. We'll take them to Fort Robinson and then take up finding Grosbeck."

"I want one day to have my wedding."

"You can have whatever time you want."

"Good. We will go that direction in the morning."

"We'll need to take turns watching for the whiskey man's return," said Slocum.

Noko agreed.

Mid-afternoon, one of the squaws ran over and told Slocum that Waites was returning—she'd heard him singing coming up the road.

When Waites arrived, both Slocum and Noko stepped out and held him at gunpoint.

"What's happened?" the man asked, obviously drunk.

"Hands high and get off the horse. Where did Grosbeck go?"

"North Platte, to rob a bank. Why?"

"Thanks. Now, put your hands behind your back."

"What for?"

"We're tying your hands behind you, and then we're hanging you for killing my friend Sam and stealing my horses."

"Hangin' me?"

"Yes, four of your friends are already in God's hands."

"Oh, God, save me. I'm a sinner, but I don't deserve to hang."

"No, you deserve to hang. Find another rope," Slocum said to his partner.

"No!" Waites cried.

"Shut up or I'll gag you."

Noko returned with a rope.

"Sit down," Slocum ordered the man and began fashioning a noose. The women were busy stacking things they wanted hauled back with them. Slocum's attention was on the noose. If Grosbeck intended to rob a bank in North Platte, maybe he could wire the law from the fort and warn officials down there in time to stop him.

He shook his head. He didn't know if the law there had any warrants to hold Grosbeck and his gang, before he completed his handicraft on the bank.

"Here, Noko. Go set it up. I'll bring him and his horse."

He took Waites roughly by the collar, and Snow brought his horse. Noko set the rope over the crossbar and then put the noose around Waites's neck, with him seated on his saddle. The noose strung on him, Slocum asked if he had any words.

"May you think about my poor mother in Abilene who I send support money to—will you think about my three children in Kansas who I provide money for—think about my lovely sister, Carla, who is a whore in Omaha, and God deliver me from this unfair sentence."

Slocum nodded at Noko, and he beat the horse on the butt. The rope cinched up with a squeak, and the outlaw's neck cracked aloud. He swung in death's arms, and the squaws chanted and stomp danced around the corpse in celebration of his death.

Waites's pockets yielded forty dollars and some change, and Slocum gave it all to Noko. His man shook his head, but he accepted it. "I will give this to Swan."

Slocum agreed. The outlaw horses could only carry so much. He expected them to ride, too, so they decided to stash the rest of what the women were saving in a cabin they wouldn't burn when they set fire to the rest. The women could come back with wagons for what they couldn't take with them. In the morning, they left three cabins burning hard and consuming the corpses of the gang. Of course, Slocum knew Grosbeck could find more gang members, but these were his most loyal. And they were no more.

Two days later, they arrived at Fort Robinson. The women had reunions. Noko told Slocum he would get married while they were there. Then Slocum and Snow rode over to the military to get Snow back with her people, who were under the army's command.

A captain met them and told them to take seats. Slocum explained that Snow was separated from her tribe and had been under his protection until she was kidnapped and then rescued. She wished to rejoin her father.

"We get tribe members every few days who come to rejoin their people. Yes, I will give her permission to rejoin them. I am sure her father will be glad to see her. Thanks for your effort to get her here." He shook Slocum's hand.

After they left the captain's office, he and Snow spoke softly about parting. She had forty dollars in a purse for her needs.

"I wish you good fortune in this move."

"I cannot thank you enough. I will never forget you and, also, you saving me from that terrible man. I know we must separate here. As soiled as I am, I think my people still need me. I wish you your freedom, too."

"You aren't soiled. Hold your head up proud. You're smart, educated, and you will be fine in this new life. Snow, you must lead your people in their new land. They will need a strong woman like you to do that for them."

She nodded solemnly.

He felt a pain in his chest as he went for his horse. The whole thing about moving her people south was unnecessary. Swinging into the saddle, he headed for the camp, where Noko's bride waited. Still undecided about sending the telegram to the North Platte officials, he rode into the Sioux camp only to find it in a big stir.

Swan caught him and told him to go to her lodge. Everyone had taken sides, either for Noko marrying his cousin or against it.

"It is stupid. They have been lovers for years. It will be over soon, but you can rest over there in my lodge." She gathered her buckskin skirt and started to leave, running to another site. "I won't be long."

"I'll be there."

She smiled, looking back from a distance. "Good." And then she left him.

He dismounted his buffalo horse, Sitting Bull. The return of his mount was something he really appreciated. The crop-eared gelding that he had never expected to see again had been among the other outlaws' horses. None of them had ridden him, or else they'd just dismissed him. With his ears half-off, they must have thought he was some old Indian bronc.

A bare-chested Indian walked up bold-like and acted indignant that Slocum had the horse. "White man, where did you get that horse?"

"I bought him at Fort Laramie, from a Sioux."

"I saw him at the Little Big Horn fight."

"Who rode him then?"

"A chief I did not know rode him."

"He's a good horse to ride. Bad men who killed my partner stole him. I never thought I'd see him again."

"Bullets could not kill him."

"You think so?"

"Thousands of horses died in that battle."

"I'm proud I have him."

"You are Noko's friend?"

"Yes. He's a good man."

"I am jealous you have Swan."

"She's my friend. If you want her, why don't you court her? I'll leave here in a few days. What is your name?"

"Buffalo Red."

"Buffalo Red, my name is Slocum. I'm pleased to meet you."

Slocum nodded and went on his way, grateful the big Indian wasn't mad about him staying with Swan or about his possession of the war horse. He wasn't surprised the gelding had been used at the Little Big Horn—he'd never told Buffalo Red he called the horse Sitting Bull either.

He unsaddled the roan and hobbled him, then went to take a nap. He awoke with a naked woman beside him. It was when his hand touched her bare skin that he opened his eyes and saw her smile.

"They will be married in two days."

"Good. I have some time to be with you." His palm ran over the smooth skin on her hip as he enjoyed her being there to pet.

"I sent your horse to the herd."

"Good. I don't need him. I have you."

"I want to kiss you."

He held a finger to her lips. "I want to kiss you, but a man spoke to me and said he wanted to court you."

"Who was he?"

"Buffalo Red."

"He is part of the old way." She shook her head. "That is what got my man killed."

"I think he's had time to think. He told me he was there, but he never said, 'We will win the next fight.'"

"I will listen to him, but being a dead man's wife is not easy. If I marry someone, I want him to live with me and not ride off to wars he can't win today." She leaned over and kissed him. "And he must kiss me, too."

They both laughed. In a short while, they were making

fierce love on her pallet, and Slocum forgot about anything but enjoying her body. That evening, they went to a feast celebrating the coming wedding for Noko and his cousin, Yellow Flower. A large half buffalo roasted over a great fire, turned by diligent women. Seated on the ground beside Swan, Slocum ate with his fingers, among the chattering Sioux. He felt almost alone, but the food was so good he didn't give a damn, as he recalled his days on a jerky diet. Swan brought him some fry bread, and he nodded his approval.

"I forget you don't speak Sioux."

"I'm enjoying this good food. Don't worry about me. I'll have more fun after all this than I can imagine."

She agreed.

The wedding was a happy affair. Children ran about the camp all excited. Dogs shared their enthusiasm. Swan held Slocum's arm and led him around with her head high. There was much feasting, and she found him some huckleberry jam and fresh fry bread to eat. The sweet blue berries had a tartness that his tongue enjoyed, and he decided he would weigh twenty pounds more before Noko was even married.

When the women teased Swan about the big white man she tagged along with, Swan laughed a lot. "They are only jealous I have you. Many of them don't know where you came from and how I got you."

"I understand. I think you're having lots of fun dragging me about."

"Yes, and I am over being a head-down widow, thanks to you." She threw her shoulders back, and her neat breasts pushed the deerskin dress out.

"Good."

"Where will you go after this?" she asked.

"I must find this killer who murdered Sam."

She nodded. "For now, you are my man. I want you to meet my sister. She just arrived."

Her sister, Blue Bird, shared Swan's tall frame. She had some small children with her, and her man gave Slocum a cold look when they met.

"He is not a soldier," Swan said. "He saved four Sioux women who were being held against their will by outlaws. Have you saved any of our women lately?"

The man chuckled at her obvious anger toward him for not accepting Slocum.

"Good man, I will shake your hand."

"Good. Where do you live?"

"Our village is north of here on a stream. Where do you live?"

"Under the stars."

He laughed. "Good place. I liked that better than the place I have now."

"A young woman I rescued is a Cheyenne. They are taking her people to the Indian Territory next spring."

"I have heard about that." He shook his head. "I would hate to have to go there."

"Me, too."

Swan gathered them and their children and, with her arm locked on Slocum's, took them to a place in the camp where they were fed buffalo stew and fry bread. More food to eat—all part of the camp's celebration. They used their fingers and bread to eat, then Swan found Slocum a spoon.

The day passed quickly, and the wedding was held. Noko and his bride rode off on hand-painted horses with a red circle around the right eye on each. Slocum never found out the reason for the artwork, if there was one. Having partied all day with Swan, he was grateful to be back in her tepee. Alone there, she made him undress and lie facedown. Then she sat astraddle him to massage his back muscles. Under her powerful hands, the tension in his muscles soon dissolved.

"I could pack you along to do that every day."

"Oh, I am a Sioux, and I need to be with my people, even though I have had much fun showing you off."

"I understand. I've enjoyed your pride, too. But I must go look for this killer of my friend."

"You can stay a few days more. You are just getting over the damage they did to you."

He rolled over and pulled her down to kiss her mouth. Sprawled on top of him, she laughed. "You are a real lover. I know I will miss you. But I know you, like me, have things you must do."

They made love in her bed. After her massage, as well as their sex, he slept good. The next dawn, he had one of the boys bring him his horse. He sat cross-legged in his saddle and ate the food Swan fetched for him.

"I know you will not return, so I can long for you. But I also know you think I should marry a man. It may not be Buffalo Red, but I will search hard for him."

"You'll find him."

"You sound so sure."

"I'm sure."

She stretched up, and he leaned down so she could kiss him. "For that, I am grateful."

He left the Red Cloud Agency to see if he could find Grosbeck. His venture heading south might make him vulnerable to arrest, but he couldn't let that delay his purpose. This wasn't the first time he'd been falsely accused of a crime he didn't commit. But that could be handled, too, if necessary. He simply didn't want any lengthy stall in an arrest holding him back from finding Grosbeck and settling this business between them.

He stopped over at the Borne ranch for the night, telling them about their success and Noko's wedding. Nelly had many questions and asked if the boy would ever come back to work for them.

"Yes. He likes working here and considers himself to be a modern Indian."

Bill nodded from his end of the table. "I think you know that boy well."

"He is a brave, tough, young man." Slocum dropped his head to concentrate on the rich food Nelly had served. Enough said—in the morning he'd be gone south and on his way to find Grosbeck. A needle in a haystack maybe, but he would sure try to avoid any arrest and locate him.

That night, in bed by himself he wondered how Snow was doing rejoined with her tribe. He missed her not being with him—a lot. And where was that killer Grosbeck?

13

He knew a rancher above North Platte who would help him, so the next day Slocum pushed southeast. That evening, a rancher named Hiram Yates put him and Bull up for the night. Yates, a bachelor with four Texas cowhands, was learning the ins and outs of ranching in the north country. His brand was the HYK, and he, like the rest of the displaced Lone Star cattlemen up there, couldn't believe the grass they'd found. Yates had his men busy mowing and stacking hay, so Slocum decided the man was realistic about the Nebraska winter he faced.

A friendly bunch, they asked Slocum a lot of questions while they sat around the supper table.

One young man said, "Ain't nothing wrong with Hiram's cooking, but if you ever find a nice lady that would cook, send her up here. It might help all our dispositions."

"Hell, Curly, ain't no nice lady coming up here."

"He might find one. We damn sure ain't got the time to go looking."

"Send her on," Hiram said and laughed. "We'd treat her damn nice."

"If I find one, I'll send her up here to cook for you all."

"Great," Curly said.

Next morning, he rode southeast again through the waving prairie. About dark, he found a place that looked deserted, with a sod house and corrals, way out in the middle of nowhere. When he came around the south side, a haggard young woman opened the door. She pushed the hair back from her face and looked hard at him.

When he stepped down from his saddle, her knees buckled, and she fainted.

Too late to save her fall, he swept her up in his arms and carried her inside. The main room was dimly lit, for sod houses had few windows save the open doorway. He laid her on the bed, then went to find a washcloth and some water to bathe her face.

Slow-like, she came to and blinked her eyes.

"Who are you?" he asked, with a million more questions behind his tongue.

"Diane—Stokes . . ."

"You disappeared in Kansas after a bank robbery?"

Her brows furrowed at him. "How did you know that?"

"The guy who robbed it said he was John Slocum. That's my name."

"His real name was Billy Hank Spurlock. You know him?"

Slocum shook his head. "Were you kidnapped?"

"In a way, yes. That lying bastard told me he'd marry me if I went away with him. I didn't know he was planning to rob a bank, and I wanted out desperately from my husband and my life there. He knew that, too."

"Where is Spurlock now?"

"They rode off without me. Two days ago."

"You have any food?"

She sat up, fussed with her hair. "Not much. They tied me in that chair and said good-bye. I got loose."

"What were you planning to do?"

"Hang myself."

"My God, girl!" He turned and saw the rope around the open rafter and the spilled chair.

"Rope broke."

"Thank God that it did."

"Easy for you to say. I'm not going back to Kansas. I'm not going to work in a brothel, and I'm not going to be gang-raped by outlaws again, either."

"Let's find some food from my saddlebags and we can fix something to eat. Then I'm taking you to a nice ranch tomorrow that needs you. You can cook, can't you?"

"Sure. Why?"

"They want a woman cook and they'll treat you nice."

"I don't have any clothes. I have nothing."

"They'll accept you for who you are and hide your identity."

"How do you know them?"

"Trust me, I know people, Diane. I need to know where those bank robbers went."

"What will you do with them?"

"Clear my damn name, for one thing."

"I understand. I'll meet these men who need a cook. But I ain't saying I'll stay there."

"It's the perfect place to stay."

"I'll have to see. Maybe I can find a better rope." By this time, they were beside his horse, and he took out some provisions.

"Here's some real coffee. Enough brown beans to have a meal. An onion I got from their garden and some bacon. Now, go be a cook. I'll hobble Bull and be along in a few minutes."

Her hands full, she simply stood there. "Damn, I ain't

had any Arbuckle coffee since I left Kansas. You bend over, so I can kiss you."

"Good. I need to be kissed." He grabbed her up and hugged groceries and all in their kiss.

"You work on that ranch?"

"No, ma'am, but you'll like them."

"Slocum, I can't hardly believe a ranch would hire me to cook for them."

"This one would and you'll see tomorrow evening."

"Where were you headed anyway, coming by here?" she asked.

"I was trying to cut off some other bank robbers who were going to rob the North Platte Bank. They looked at it and decided it might be too damn tough a deal for them to handle. Billy Hank thought it would be a good to place to get shot up."

He finished hobbling Bull so he could graze. "He probably was wise not to hold up another bank and use my damn name."

He took her back to the house. "They all rape you?"

"The last night. Every one of them. There's seven of them. Tied me on the damn bed and had their fun. I finally fainted, and they still raped me."

"Damn their worthless hides. Wish I'd got here sooner. Well, I have a better place for you. Now get to cooking." He looked over at her. "Weren't there eleven in the bank?"

"Back then there were. Harold broke his neck falling off a bucking horse the second day. Garcia got to fighting with a whore in Hayes over the price she charged him. She pushed him out the second-story window and he broke his back in the fall. Neal died from eating poison mushrooms. Thank God, there were only seven here that night."

He hugged her shoulder. "I'm sorry. Those bastards need to be hung."

"Instead of me."

"Right, get that out of your mind."

She halfheartedly agreed and went to cooking. Her coffee was good, and the bacon and beans were wonderful. When they'd finished, she put their dirty dishes on the dry sink. "The next fool comes by can wash them. You have any soap?"

"Sure. You need some?"

"I have needed some since he took me from the house, behind him on his saddle, and we rode like hell for Hayes."

Slocum went to his saddlebags, fetched the soap and a towel, and handed them to her.

"You good at soaping backs?"

"I have been known to do that quite well."

"The wind is up, and the mill's pumping good enough. I've used it a time or two, but without soap you don't get clean. Let me warn you, the water is damn cold."

They both undressed, and she swung the pipe over to wash under the outflow. She had a neatly shaped body, stark white in the setting sunlight. Her breasts were not too large and were topped with silver dollar–size nipples, and they sure looked tempting to squeeze. She walked back to where he stood undressed, waiting for her.

The spout of water doused her down and she gave a soft gasp, "Oh."

He handed her the soap, and she used a rag to soap up. He lathered the bar and his hands to soap her back and then her lovely derriere. She hadn't lied. The water was damn near icy, and he was getting splashed with it while she washed. The job was a tough one, but someone had to do it. He slid his hands under her arms, reached around, and squeezed her bare breasts.

"Anyone ever tell you that you are lovely?"

"No one ever did that."

The cold water cascaded down his back, but he didn't

care. She leaned back into the flying water going down over her head and he leaned in and kissed her. She twisted around until she hugged him to her. "My God, Slocum, I am real glad that rope broke."

He pressed his flank against her and agreed. "It was our day."

"Reach up and swing that pipe back over the tank. I'm freezing."

He did, and the surge of the water from the pipe soon spilled into the large tank. They dried themselves on his towel until it was too wet to dry either one, but the low humidity dried them as they ran for the house. She fluffed her hair to try to dry it, and laughed.

"Why didn't I marry you?" she asked. "You are an exciting, don't-give-a-damn man."

"You probably married right. He just went wrong."

She shook her head. "It wasn't right. He sired children in other women and lied to me."

"Hey, you want to do this, or forget it?"

"Do it. What have I to lose? You've been lots of fun so far."

"Get on the bed. I'm coming."

She held her arms out to receive him. His knee on the bed, he knew this would be nice. The physical energy in their naked connection spun them into a whirlpool that took them to high mountain peaks and down slick snowslides to the end. Both were breathless and completely exhausted on their backs side by side, squeezing each other's hand.

They slept locked together and woke to more relations in the predawn. Dressed, and after a breakfast of cheese, crackers, and coffee, they saddled up and threw her few things in a carpetbag that he tied on his saddle horn. He lifted her up behind the cantle, and they set out on Bull for Hiram Yates's HKP Ranch.

It was dark when they arrived, and Hiram hailed Slocum from the house. "That you, Slocum?"

"Yeah. I found you a cook."

A cheer went up, and the crew shouted and ran out of the house to see her. She pulled on his shirtsleeve. "You sure I'm going to be safe here?"

"A little boisterous now, but they're great guys."

He swung her down and stepped off his horse. "Gentlemen, this is Diane Stokes. She needs a job and I fetched her for your cook."

"Howdy, ma'am, we're sure proud to have you here." Hiram stepped forward with his Stetson in his hand. "The boys and I are shocked. Slocum said he'd look for a cook for us, and now he is back in just two days. We'll fix private quarters for you to get some peace and quiet. And as pretty as you are, we'll sure all be proud to have you here."

She chewed on her lower lip, then spoke up. "Mr. Yates, it shall be my pleasure to be your cook."

A cheer went up from the men on the porch.

She nodded to them, and Slocum herded her into the house.

"Better look it over, this is your kitchen and dining hall."

"They act pleased I came." She ran her fingers across the dry sink.

He nodded. "They will be pleased."

"I owe you a lot. Only you could have done this for me."

"I'll explain your situation to Hiram. You'll be safe here. If it was me, I'd change my name."

"I never even thought of that."

"They'll understand."

"Slocum, I know you won't come back, but I appreciate all you've done."

Hiram joined them. "Until we get a private room built, you can sleep in my bed in there."

"I won't take your bed."

"Yes, you will." He smiled. "Slocum, you did well. We'll care for her."

"There are some mean men in her past, who treated her badly, but her heart is good and she'll treat you like kings."

"I have some clean sheets for your bed," Hiram said.

Later, Slocum slept alone in his own bedroll.

In the morning Diane made them breakfast of pancakes, syrup, and oatmeal. She also told Hiram she'd make him a list of groceries she'd like to have bought.

"Anything you need, we'll go get," Hiram said. "Your food is wonderful."

"Well, you guys owe me. See you again sometime," Slocum said. He winked at her and she winked back. The ranch had a cook, and he was off to find Grosbeck.

He reached the edge of North Platte in two hard days' riding and stopped off at Verna Lee's HHH ranch. She was a large woman in her late forties. Her beauty still shone when she came out on the porch and waved at him to get up there.

"Slocum, where have you been?"

"Oh, here and there. I'm looking for an outlaw named Grosbeck. He shot my friend." Holding Verna Lee in his arms, he hugged and kissed her.

"I've not heard of him before."

"He operated up near Fort Robinson."

"Oh, that's why. That's a far piece from here."

"They say he's around here to rob a local bank."

"What does he look like?"

"A big man, swarthy complexion. He's not Mexican or Indian. A bully and worthless."

"He killed your friend?"

"Thought he had me, too. He left me for dead."

"Harley, put his horse up and grain him. He's my guest."

She dismissed her man, who'd come to check on who stopped by, and he took Bull away to care for him.

Her arm over his shoulder, Verna Lee guided him inside the house with a great breast poked in his side. Once they were inside, she took his hat and hung it on the wall hook.

Her hand was out for his six-gun, and he unbuckled it with a grin. He redid the buckle and hung it on the next peg.

"You sure won't need to shoot me, darling. Or force me to go to bed with you." She smiled.

"Not today. You know some men I can hire to look for this guy around town?"

"I'll send someone to town and have them here after supper. Is that soon enough?"

"Absolutely."

She kissed him and let him up the wide, curving staircase to the four-poster bed. "Wait a minute, I need to tell my housekeeper about those men you need. Take off your clothes and relax."

From the upstairs railing, she spoke to a person she called Adelle and rattled off some names for her to have there that evening—she had work for them to do. The voice from downstairs replied that she'd do that. Then, in a rustle of her stiff dress, Verna Lee reappeared in the bedroom.

"My dear. My dear, I was all ready to take a nap, when I saw you come riding down the road. Land's sakes, I didn't need any sleep, if you're going to entertain me."

He gathered her in his arms and kissed her. A bedful of woman, she could rouse any man into enjoying her ample body. A widow twice over, she owned almost an empire of grass north of the Platte River. His fingers worked on the small buttons to free her of the dress, and she told him how much she had missed him and asked when he would settle down there and let her spoil him in exchange for his services.

"My land, darlin', some two-bit outlaw robbed a bank in

Abilene and used my name. That has a Denver detective agency on my tracks looking for me, and then this Grosbeck, who killed Sam Clover, is planning to rob another bank here."

She stepped out of the dress and waved his concerns away. "If they are in the area, you'll soon know those men's whereabouts."

All kissy-faced, her voluptuous body was soon on her back atop the bed. A soft Nebraska wind swept his bare skin as he stood over her. He closed his eyes and imagined pleasure's path ahead, then put his knee on the bed. Here comes excitement and lots of womanhood that quickly would turn into a raging volcano. Hold on to his butt, this would be a real ride, and he went forth.

Her cries aloud and movements swirled his mind and gave his muscles the strength to please her. The pleasure of riding high, with her under his muscle-corded belly, ignited the lightning charges of a powerful storm. Their lovemaking went long and ended like a soaring Mexican rocket, bursting in a shower of stars that fell to the ground.

They both napped afterward.

Then he bathed and shaved while she dressed. After dressing, she took charge of the supper event as if a king might arrive any moment and things must be just so to suit him. After they ate, the men she'd sent for arrived, and she had Slocum describe the man he looked for.

The men seated around the room consisted of a mustached gambler, Riley Cornwall; Herb Knight, a man in his forties who owned the largest saloon in town; and finally, Coburt Flanagan, a thin man with a hard face who looked like he had little patience for anyone in his way.

Slocum began, "Grosbeck is a big man, graying hair, and wears a vest, plus a blue kerchief. His hat was once an expensive one, and he may have a new one by now. He's loud and a bully. His men, I have never really seen, so they would be just hard cases. He operates a ring of holdup men committing robbery, horse stealing, plus raping white women and squaws.

"Billy Hank Spurlock is the one who robbed the Abilene, Kansas, bank and told them he was me. I have never met the man, but would silence him for his usage of my name during that robbery."

The men chuckled.

"There's a poster on him at the sheriff's office," Flanagan said. "He's another big man. I haven't seen him in town, but I believe the first man you mentioned—Grosbeck—is over in Willows right now. That's a camp of shacks and lodges of Indian whores, trash, and bums down on the Platte."

The other two nodded.

"This Spurlock, you've never seen him?" Cornwall asked.

"No. He kidnapped a woman and, in the end, let his gang of men rape her."

"Ever learn why he used your name during the robbery?"

Slocum shook his head. "I've never met him as far as I know, but he wanted them to think it was me."

"I can get any poster on him that Sheriff Miles has and explain to Lloyd that you aren't him," the saloon man said.

Verna Lee thanked him and then turned to Slocum. "That should lower the pressure on you,"

"It will a lot. Thanks."

"I can be ready anytime to go down there in those hovels and try to find Grosbeck," Flanagan offered. "It's a pretty tough place."

"I can imagine. Sunup tomorrow?" Slocum asked.

"Meet me at Knight's Texas Saloon. I'll be on the porch."

"I'll do that."

"When you two come back, I'll have a poster for this guy who uses your name—Spurlock, wasn't it?" asked Cornwall.

"Yes, that's the one he used when he wasn't Slocum."

"You all have things to do," she said. "Like I said earlier, this man is a longtime friend and what he says is the truth. My late husband, Dower, and Slocum brought cattle up the Chisholm Trail together. For all his past service to me, I'd do anything he needs to make things happen."

The others nodded and shook Slocum's hand, wishing him success in his endeavor. When they left, each one hugged Verna Lee.

"Was that the help you needed?" she asked when they had ridden off.

"Exactly. Thanks a lot. I'll find them. If I can locate Grosbeck and settle with him, it will be something over for me."

"No telling where Spurlock could be. But Flanagan is a good man and has handled some of my problems for me. He's tough, too."

"I can see that. We better get some sleep. Morning is going to come early for me."

"Will four in the morning be early enough?"

"Fine."

"I'll get things set. You go upstairs and don't fall asleep before I get there."

"Yes, ma'am."

"Well, knowing your sugar foot ways, it might be your last night to sleep with me for a long while."

"Yes, ma'am."

"Go on."

They had a quick encounter in bed, and he had no trouble seeking sleep. But the wakeup was harder to shake. He dressed and went down to eat the meal Verna Lee's housekeeper, Adelle, had fixed. Verna Lee was there to talk to him, and they had a short conversation.

"I hope you find him today."

"Me, too. Great food, Adelle. And thanks for all your help, Verna Lee. This was great."

"Glad you like it. Come back again. We have lots of food."

"Amen to that," Verna Lee said.

"Will you come back?" Adelle asked.

"Depends. If I get him, I will. Otherwise, I'll be on his trail."

"I understand. Good luck," Verna Lee said. "Adelle and I will be glad if you can return." She smiled.

"I will, if I can." He rose, and she traipsed behind him in her robe. His pistol strapped on and his hat on his head, he kissed her and went out the front door. Her man stood at the yard gate with Bull's reins. Slocum thanked him and checked the girth. Satisfied, he swung on board and touched his hat brim to Verna Lee on the dark porch and her man standing nearby.

On the road, he short loped to the bridge and crossed the river flowing like ink in the starlight. He soon was at the saloon, and Flanagan came off the porch to meet him. The thin man unhitched his horse and then in a low voice said, "I believe he's there right now."

"Sounds good."

They rode down into the head-high willows area along the river that held shacks, tents, and lots of derelicts. Some clotheslines were strung, so they were careful not to get unhorsed by them. Flanagan dismounted and said they should go on foot from there. Slocum stepped down and tested his pistol to be certain it would easily come free of his holster. He nodded to Flanagan and took the lead.

The tent-shack Flanagan pointed to sat in the starlight. There were some horses snoring in a pole corral nearby.

Flanagan spoke softly. "According to my information, there are three men and a woman in there. I'll go around front."

"Let me go. I'll kick in the door and order them to get up. Hands high."

"All right. I'll watch, so they don't get out this side."

"Good. They will either wilt or fight."

Flanagan agreed.

Slocum moved around the front and stepped to the door. With his boot he smashed it in. "Hands high or die."

"Fuck you!" Followed by the flash of a shot, so Slocum thumbed back his hammer and fired three in that direction. A hysterical, naked woman ran out screaming past him. Flanagan was shooting from out back. Slocum knew he couldn't see anything in the cave-like house, so he ran around the shed. Flanagan was on the ground, and he knelt beside him.

"You hit bad?"

"I don't think so, but it damn sure hurts a lot."

"Can you ride a horse?"

"With help."

"Did that big guy come by you?" asked Slocum.

"Yeah. He shot me. I think I winged him."

"Good. I'll get you to the doctor. I'm going after our horses."

He hurried to get them, afraid the outlaws might have left on them. But the horses were there. He unhitched them and ran back.

In the darkness, he helped Flanagan to his feet and helped load him in the saddle, then Slocum took off for medical help leading the thin man's horse. Flanagan was still hanging on when they reached the edge of town.

"Where's a doctor?" Slocum asked some laborers headed for work.

"Two blocks down on the right."

"Thanks." He hurried on to stop before a two-story dark house with a sign that said DOCTOR.

He dismounted and told Flanagan to stay in the saddle. "Help! I have a man shot out here. Help me."

A man in a nightcap stuck his head out an upstairs window. "I'm coming down. Right now."

Some passersby took Flanagan off the horse and carried him up the front steps. By this time, the doctor was unlocking the door, so they took him inside, where one lamp was lit.

"Who did this?"

"An outlaw named Grosbeck and two of his men," said Slocum.

The law arrived about then. "What happened?"

"Flanagan and I were about to arrest an outlaw named Grosbeck. He came out shooting, shot Flanagan, then ran."

"He have a horse?"

"He didn't get his own. They were still out front."

"I'll get some men and go see if I can find him."

"Good. I'll join you as soon as I see about Flanagan. My name's Slocum. Verna Lee will vouch for me."

"You have a description?"

"Big man. Dark complexion."

"You know him?"

"Yes, he's been running wild over northwest Nebraska raping women and robbing stages."

"I've seen some of those wanted posters. I'll be up there shortly."

"Let me check on Flanagan," Slocum said, then stepped inside.

"Go ahead. We'll get ready to go," the deputy said.

Flanagan sat on top of the operating table, with his pant leg split and the bloody wound gaping.

The doctor made him lie down so he could examine it, then shook his head and spoke to Slocum. "It looks like a simple wound. After we get the bullet out, we'll try to stop the bleeding and then he should be all right."

"Thanks. Someone get the word to Verna Lee that he was wounded. She'll want to know. I'm going back to help the deputy."

"We can get that done," a man promised him.

"Good. Take care of him. He's brave man."

He ran to get on Bull and charged off to find the deputy. He was soon back in Willows, and the first women he saw in a group, he reined up beside them.

"Have you seen any hatless men running around here?"

"Yes. They shot at a few people and ran back west. A couple of men chased them with guns. There, hear those shots?"

With a thanks and a nod, Slocum hurried westward. He came up on two men with smoking revolvers behind a turned over wagon. Short of them, he set Bull down in a sliding stop, dismounted, and joined them.

"How many shooters are there?"

"Two. They shot at some women. Made Jeb and me mad."

"You boys have ammo?"

"No."

"There are some forty-five cartridges in my saddlebags."

"Good, we can use them. I'll get them, Jeb."

"Think they're still there?" Slocum asked Jeb.

"They were shooting from behind that cart."

"I'll empty my six-gun into it and see what happens."

"I can watch through a crack. Fire away."

Slocum fast-fired his gun into the cart area, from right to left. One of the shooters screamed he was hit. Busy shucking casings, Slocum nodded. "Now where is his partner?"

"I hear a horse taking off. He may be getting away from us."

His gun reloaded, Slocum said, "You hold that wounded guy for the deputy. He'll be here soon."

"We can damn sure do that," Jeb's partner said and handed Slocum the half-empty cartridge box. He tossed it inside his saddlebags, then mounted up. The men thanked him as he urged Bull around the wagon and headed westward. As he slapped Bull on the butt with his handgun, they burst through the willows. He saw the back end of a horse with a hatless rider headed for higher ground. Convinced that was his man, he took after him in hot pursuit.

The deep sand held the big horse back some, but they were soon up on the prairie and racing after their quarry. It was obvious to Slocum that the outlaw was running his bay horse for all he was worth and that the mount would soon bottom out. Bull was a damn sight tougher than most horses, and he was gaining on the rider that looked like Grosbeck. Every hundred yards, the distance between the two riders became less. Obviously, Grosbeck had emptied his pistol, because he had holstered it.

Slocum grew more confident with every minute ticking by, as the bay horse was beginning to lose his stride and Bull drew closer. Soon he was at the bay's tail, and Slocum stood in the stirrups. Being a buffalo horse, Bull had no fear of running past the bay, like most horses would have had. When things were right, Slocum dove for the fleeing man's shoulders, threw his arms around him, and took him off the horse. Hand on the back of his head, he plowed Grosbeck's face hard in the grass and dirt for a long ways. Skidding on his nose and mouth, sliding over the vegetation and piles of dirt from the gopher mounds, he tried to curse Slocum.

When they at last stopped, he jerked Grosbeck around onto his back and slammed him in his dirty bloody face with a right. The blow was so hard it made Grosbeck's head strike the ground. Unsteady, Slocum managed to stand and regain his breath.

"Get up! I'm going to pound the piss out of you. You don't have no ax handle–wielding help here this time. You ain't sitting your damn horse on some ridge watching me get beat to death. Get up!"

He gave the groaning outlaw a flying kick in the ham of

his leg. The man moaned and got up on his knees. This time Slocum kicked him in the belly and drove the wind out of him. He fell over backward and groaned, holding his guts.

With a handful of his greasy hair, Slocum raised him up on his knees; then he smashed him in the face with a hard right hand. "That was for Snow, you sumbitch. I intend to beat you senseless for what you did to her."

Cowering on the ground and holding his hands up to protect himself from any more blows, he cried out, "You're killing me. You're killing me."

"You killed lots of good men and women. You can plead, cry, whatever, but I have no use for you."

A posse was coming on horseback across the sweeping prairie. Maybe two dozen men in suits and some dressed in workers' clothing were riding hard toward him. That might spare the worthless piece of shit being killed by his own bare hands.

"We came as quick as we could," the deputy said in a flying dismount. "The one you shot is dead back there in the camp. I'm surprised this one's still alive. There was another one shot earlier, and he's dead, too. Reckon you got the whole gang."

"I simply hope Flanagan is going to be all right."

"So do we. Get him in irons and into the country jail," the lawman said to his assistants. "And, thanks, Slocum. Those men back there thanked you for giving them shells, too."

He nodded that he heard him. His right hand ached from hitting Grosbeck so damn hard. Maybe Verna Lee would soak his fist and make it hurt less. Better go that way and get rested. Billy Hank Spurlock might show up next. He'd get that sorry outfit, too.

They had bloody-faced Grosbeck in the saddle with his hands chained to the saddle horn.

"I'll get you, you sumbitch," he growled. "You wait and see. Your ass will be in a million parts."

Slocum gritted his teeth. He wanted to blow him to kingdom come with his pistol—that son of a bitch didn't deserve to live another day on this earth. Slocum told them to go on, he didn't want to hear another word out of that damn Grosbeck or he'd kill him.

He set the horse for Verna Lee's place. When he reached her front gate, she ran to meet him, carrying her dress hem

"You all right?" She was beside him to ease him off the horse. In that movement, she must have seen his swollen fist, and she grasped it. "You broke it?"

He forced a smile. "You should see the other guy."

"Let's get you in the house."

"Take care of his horse," she said to her man. Then, like a mother hen, she herded him up the stairs and into the great house.

"You got him?"

"He's in jail. They say his two men are dead. Flanagan was shot in the leg. I hope he's all right."

"I'll send someone in to check on him. You need to see a doctor."

"We'll soak it. I've done this before. Boy, it really felt good to smash that bastard for all he'd done to people."

"Adelle, draw him a hot bath."

"I'll get that done. Have you eaten lately?" her housekeeper asked as Verna Lee undid his holster, rebuckled it, and put it on the peg.

"I had breakfast."

"I'll have you some food shortly." In a swirl of skirts, Adelle hurried off toward the kitchen.

He rolled his swollen hand in the palm of the other one. That damn sure hurt.

Verna Lee set him down in a Morris chair and went to the walnut cabinet, took out a glass, and poured him a double shot of some high-priced whiskey.

"This should help you some."

He tossed it down and made a deep sound. "Ah, bound to help someplace."

They both laughed. After he ate and bathed and downed two more doubles, she put him to bed. He woke up the next morning and realized his right hand was still swollen and sore. But Grosbeck was in jail.

Verna Lee swept into the bedroom and opened the curtains to let the light shine in. "Flanagan appears to be doing fine, they say."

Seated on the side of the bed, running his fingers through his too-long hair, he nodded. "That's good news. No word on the outlaw Spurlock?"

"No one sent me word, and those other two men I had over find out many things that are going on. Though Flanagan is the best, and he'll be, like you, out for a few days."

"My hand gets a little better, I want to go see him and thank him for helping me."

His hand was so sore she had to help him dress. But at last, they went downstairs to breakfast.

Adelle looked up from doing some food preparation. "I was about to haul your food upstairs. You feel all right?"

"Doing fine."

"No, you're not." Verna Lee shook her head over his statement. "His hand is so swollen he can't even button his own clothes."

Adelle nodded like she understood his condition.

"Thanks. I have two fine ladies concerned about me. I should get well real quick." He took a place at the table, and the two fussed over him.

"No, you will probably get in a bigger fight with another outlaw," Verna Lee said in disgust.

He used his left hand to raise a steaming mug to taste

Adelle's coffee. "Mighty fine. Even better since I didn't have to make it."

They laughed at his words. After breakfast, they went to putting hot compresses on his battered hand. The skin still felt ready to bust, but it helped a lot.

He napped in the afternoon, waking up when he rolled over wrong on the hand. But the day was pleasant, and when he went downstairs for supper the aroma of Adelle's cooking filled the house.

The county sheriff dropped by to meet him. Lloyd Miles was a man in his forties with a great mustache and had not missed many meals. He was a man who obviously took charge, and right off he apologized for being in Kearny bringing a prisoner back for trial at the time of Grosbeck's arrest.

"No problem, it gave us our chance to capture Grosbeck. He'd gotten away too many times. Everyone was a big help. They came with a big posse in less than an hour. I couldn't believe they could come that fast."

"Folks back law and order out here. We want a place where settlers can live and farm safely, so more will come. We have the rich land, and usually the rainfall, to be the garden of this earth. We don't need the likes of him running around loose."

"There is a second outlaw, Billy Hank Spurlock, that held up a bank in Abilene and used my name."

"Verna Lee told me, and I wired that sheriff's office down there and told him what happened. He told me he'd make new wanted posters and to tell you that you were off the hook."

"That sounds wonderful."

"I'm much obliged for your actions. Those posse men said that if you hadn't persisted, he'd've got away again."

"Can I pour you gentlemen a drink to celebrate?" Verna Lee asked

"Verna Lee, you know I always enjoy some of that good whiskey you keep in the walnut cabinet," Sheriff Miles said. "Best booze in the county."

Slocum agreed.

After the drink, the sheriff left, and Slocum thanked Verna Lee.

"No problem, big man." She came and sat on the arm of his chair. "Miles is a real lawman, and he leads the forces around here. As long as people elect men like him, we'll have law and order in this county."

Slocum agreed.

As the days passed, his hand healed. While still not a hundred percent recovered, he could use his Colt and fire it. The two of them had long sessions in bed, and Verna Lee told him she might keep him prisoner so he couldn't leave.

Flanagan came out in a buckboard to see him. The man was on crutches, but he tied off the team and clambered down with sticks under his arms, then propelled himself on them to the porch.

"Need some help?" Slocum asked.

"No. No, I'll get up there."

"What brings you out here today?" There was a hint of fall in the cool wind pumping water real steady from Verna Lee's windmill.

"Let's go inside," Flanagan said.

Slocum held open the door, and the man hobbled into the room and spoke to Verna Lee, who was drying her hands on a tea towel.

"You men have things to say. I'll make some coffee. Go set in the living room chairs."

"Thanks, Verna," Slocum said.

Flanagan took a seat and acted relieved to be there. "I come to tell you I picked up word from a reliable source that Spurlock was staying in the Ogallala area. Not certain about his exact location. I wired the sheriff there. His name is Woolsey, and he said if Spurlock was there he hadn't heard about him. But he's around there, according to my informants."

"They have my name off the wanted posters, but he needs to be run down. My hand's getting better. I should go there and see if I can find him before he dens up for the winter."

"Wish I could go along, but I'll be a while yet and on these damn crutches. I'd not be worth much to you."

"Thanks for thinking of me. I'll get organized and go see what I can find. Thanks, Flanagan, it's been great working with you."

"Shame we can't tackle him together. I'd like to be there when you catch him."

"I hope I can."

"Adelle will have lunch shortly," Verna Lee announced.

"Well, by damn, I can still eat," Flanagan said. "This leg ain't stopped that, too."

They went in the dining room and had an enjoyable lunch, and then Flanagan left. After he drove off, Verna Lee stood by the front window and looked out at the rolling scenery. Slocum knew she wanted something and was working up her nerve to ask for it.

She turned to face him. "There is no way to get you to stay here. I know that. It always saddens me when you leave. But if you ever need money or anything, wire me. My finances are solid, and I'd be more than glad to help you, just in case you need it."

He got out of the chair and stood behind her. "You know all the things that tag along behind me. I can't stay here long. Plus, rascals like Spurlock shouldn't be running around planning more robberies. He'll kill some innocent people pulling off his next crime.

"I better get over there. I'll leave in the morning." He

hugged her from behind. "You are a great, sweet woman, and I'd not have healed without your care."

When she turned to bury her face in his shoulder, tears spilled down her cheeks. "I knew when Flanagan came today, he'd have news for you."

"Thanks." He squeezed her tight. Morning would come early. Too damn early.

He wore the new sheepskin-lined leather coat she'd had made for him. In the chill of the morning, he set Bull on the way west with an empty place in his heart for a great woman. He had a cold notion that winter was about to sweep down the face of the Rockies and smother the plains and him in snow.

When he reached Ogallala, he went by the sheriff's office and spoke to the chief deputy, Reb Corning. The sheriff had gone to Denver by train to return a murderer apprehended there. He was due back any day.

Corning had no idea where Spurlock might be hiding. That left Slocum to look for someone who knew his whereabouts. He took a room in a boardinghouse, put Bull up in a livery, and began combing bars for people who might have heard of his man. He played some dime-limit poker with unemployed teamsters, cowhands headed back for Texas, and a few of the whiskerinos that inhabited such Western towns. He learned lots about things going on, but no one knew anything about Billy Hank Spurlock.

Then a scruffily dressed man stopped him in the cold wind on the porch of Dewey's Saloon one mid-morning.

"You Slocum?"

"That's me. Who're you?"

"Grim's my name. This guy Spurlock you been asking about . . ." The man cut his gaze around to be certain he'd not be overheard. "What's he worth to you?"

"To find him? Ten bucks."

"He's denned up at the G Bar 9 ranch. Old man Sawyer knew him from before in Texas. If you tell him I sent you, he'll murder me, so don't. He's been out there lounging around." Grim shut up and let a drunk stagger past them before he spoke again. "Jenny Doll Sawyer is fucking him. That's the old man's wild-ass daughter."

"You know her?" Slocum was about to laugh.

"Gawdamn right I do, and every mole on her body. I was good enough for her until that sumbitch showed up. She knew him from Texas also."

Slocum paid him a ten-dollar gold piece. "How hard is that place to find?"

"It's ten, twelve miles north of here. Just off the main road and west a mile. They've got a sign points that way. Oh, and thanks. I appreciate this money, but don't ever mention my name up there."

"I sure won't."

Slocum had made a few friendships with locals, and he checked out what Grim had told him with Tom McCall, a freighter he played cards with and trusted.

Tom bobbed his head. "Oh, yeah. I never thought about him being up there at the G Bar 9. It belongs to Old Man Sawyer. His daughter is a wild bitch."

"I may ride up there tomorrow."

"Hey, I'd go along. I know the old man. He come up here a few years ago from Texas. That daughter of his ain't bad-looking, but she's a real rip."

"This guy who told me about her said he knew every mole on her body."

"I don't doubt that he's seen all of her." McCall laughed over the notion. "He ain't the only one either."

"Let's ride out before dawn."

McCall stuck his hand out and shook Slocum's paw.

Slocum went on up to play more ten-cent poker. Cheap entertainment, and you couldn't lose much or win much, but they were mostly nice guys. Tom McCall was one of the best. He had some business to attend to, so he bowed out of playing that day.

By late afternoon, Slocum was ahead five or so dollars and taking lots of razzing about all his big wins. Things were calm in the town, and he was enjoying the unthreatening peace of the time. His hand was mending more by the day. His plans to go look for Spurlock also made him feel confident that the bank robber could be brought in.

14

Slocum and Tom rode out before the sun cracked the eastern side of Ogallala's horizon. Tom asked him about the roan horse. Slocum told him how he ran down Grosbeck and took him out of the saddle.

"Not many horses will run past another, I know that. But the Indians taught him to do that hunting buffalo."

Tom shook his head. "I can see he's one powerful horse. You got a real bargain there."

"I'm lucky to have him. Grosbeck stole him when they killed Sam and beat me up. I found him in among his horses. I figure they thought he was some old Indian bronc and no one wanted any part of him. If they'd ever rode him, they'd have took him for themselves."

"You were damn lucky about that. This is where Sawyer's ranch land starts. We're still a ways from his headquarters. He owns lots of country. He sold a big place in south Texas and bought all this up here. Of course, he bought it for a song back then. Who in the hell even wanted it back then? But he knew cattle would do good on the grass up here."

"Do you know Spurlock on sight?"

"I saw him a few years ago in Texas. I think I'd know him."

"Where in the hell did he get my name to use?"

"No telling." McCall was tickled and laughed. "Are there any earlier wanted posters out on you?"

"There could be."

McCall nodded his head. "I bet that's where he found it."

"Maybe I can learn that from him."

"Chances are good you will."

"Tell Sawyer I'm Smith." Slocum laughed.

"I bet he don't know you. We top that next rise, we can probably see the headquarters."

They hustled their horses to the top and reined up. Slocum could see the layout of log buildings, many large corrals, and fenced haystacks. They were still at a good distance, and even the horses only looked like dots on a page.

When they rode up to the ranch house, Slocum wanted eyes in the back of his head. The old man came out—white whiskers and all. A sawed-off guy, long past fifty, and he wore a long-barrel Colt in a cross-draw holster.

"That you, Tom McCall?"

"It is, Mr. Sawyer. How have you been? Oh, this is John Smith, a good friend of mine." McCall dismounted, and so did Slocum.

"Good to meet you." He nodded at Slocum. "Come in the house. I don't catch much company out here. Your folks still in Texas, Tom?"

"No, they both passed away over the past two years."

"I get a letter or two from Texas. I didn't hear about that. Sorry, I knew them well. You two have a chair. What brings you up here?"

When they were settled in some worn chairs, Slocum

looked the place over. There were some big elk horns over the fireplace mantel, rifles on the wall rack, and a large painting of a woman, no doubt Sawyer's deceased wife. Tom had said he was a widower.

"I'm going to be frank with you," Tom said. "We're here on business. Billy Hank Spurlock used my friend here's name in a bank robbery. Neither one of us would have given a damn about a bank robbery, but he wants to clear his name. So we're here to arrest him and take him back to the authorities."

"He ain't here to arrest, boys. Him and Jenny Doll left two days ago headed west. I couldn't talk her out of going. She's all I have. I knew he was worthless as tits on a boar hawg, but I couldn't convince her of that. What's your real name?"

"Slocum."

"I never heard him mention it before, but that ain't surprising. Out here, I don't hear much what's going on anyway."

"Tom, she never said where they were headed even?"

He shook his head. "I figure Cheyenne or Montana."

"I'm sorry. You take care. I reckon Slocum will ride on looking for him."

"Can't say I blame you. If you find him, try not to shoot her. If she's broke, give her the fare to come back. I'll pay you double for doing it."

"You're a helluva good man, Sawyer. I'm glad I met you, and I understand your sorrow." Slocum rose and shook his hand. "It was a real pleasure meeting you."

"Hmm, an old fart sitting here hoping she'll just come home to me."

"If I can help her, I'll do that. Tom, I better head west. Thanks for your day and coming out here with me."

"Hold up. I don't have anything but a dime-raise poker game back there. I'll ride along."

"You boys need some food?"

They both shook their heads. Slocum put his hat back on, and they left the old man on the porch. In the saddle, Tom pointed the way, and they waved to Sawyer as they rode out.

"You know you don't have to ride with me?"

"I got an idea. You find him, I might please her by taking her home. She ain't bad-looking, and I figure that damn Spurlock by now has slapped her around enough she's ready for a man who treats her like a lady."

Slocum, amused by his friend's assumptions, nodded in agreement.

They stayed with some nesters that evening, a raw-boned couple existing on the edge of nothing. In the morning, Slocum paid her two dollars for their food and lodging on the dirt floor. She about cried.

Four days later, they reached Cheyenne. After putting their horses in Farris's Livery, they each bought a new shirt, underwear, socks, and pants, then went to a Chinese bathhouse to get a shave and haircut. Slocum knew a boardinghouse where they took a room, and then they had a real meal at the New York Restaurant.

After that they went barhopping, looking for a lead on Spurlock. In the Texas Bar, a guy Slocum knew said he thought Spurlock was down in the shantytown. When Tom asked if he had a redheaded woman with him, the man said, "Hell, yes."

They took a taxi to the shantytown, where they met an old derelict who wanted a handout to buy booze. In rags and unshaven for years, he reeked like piss to Slocum.

"You know where we can find Billy Hank Spurlock?"

The old man held out his dirty palm. "For fif-fifty cents, I can take you *dere*."

"Lead on. I have the money." Slocum showed him a paper dollar.

He made a wave like someone swatting gnats and turned westward. In his near barefoot shuffle, he led them through the camp. Women were hanging washed rags on their clotheslines, and many of them eyed the men's passing with distrust. Two or three shouted, "You boys want a fuck?"

Slocum waved and shook his head. "Not now."

"Well, come back," she shouted. "I got the best there is in Wyoming."

Tom smiled and under his breath said, "I can really imagine how good it is."

Slocum agreed.

"That shack there. That's where him and her live. They just came here."

Slocum handed the man the dollar. "If you're lying to me, I'll shoot you."

"No, mister. They stay there."

Slocum and Tom carefully approached the shack. Guns drawn, they circled it, but saw no sign of anyone. While Tom covered him, Slocum got up on the porch. He turned the handle on the old door, the most modern thing about the shack.

A woman in the shadows, screamed, "Don't shoot!"

His eyes were slow to adjust to the interior's shaded light, but he saw a naked woman tied to a high-backed chair. Carefully, he uncocked the pistol and holstered it.

"Jenny Doll, you all right?" Tom asked, holstering his gun. "Where the hell is Spurlock? And why are you tied up naked?"

Slocum cut her loose, and when she was free, she jumped up and went to kissing Tom. "My God, Tom, I am so glad you came for me. That sumbitch had me tied, and took my clothes with him so if I got loose I wouldn't leave. Oh, you two are my heroes for life."

"That's Slocum. Spurlock used his name in a robbery in Kansas."

"I know. He bragged to me about doing that. In case someone else come along, I'm getting a blanket to wrap up in. You two can look at me all day. But, well, strangers, that would be different."

"When is he due back?" Slocum asked while she wrapped her neat freckled form in a plaid blanket.

"Whenever he's drunk or wants my body. How did you know I was here?"

"We were at your ranch a couple days ago and spoke to your father. He told us you went with him."

"Oh, yeah. He told me Spurlock was worthless and would hurt me before it was over."

Tom hugged her. "Do you think after all this you're ready to settle down up there and be a married woman?"

She threw her head back and blinked in disbelief at him. "Tom McCall, after all this, you'd take me for your wife?"

"Damnit, Jenny Doll, I didn't ride clear out here for any other reason."

"Why, I may have his baby in me."

"Jenny Doll, I won't know him from my own I aim to make with you. Now it's time you grew up and became a wife and took over that ranch."

She made a puzzled face. "He hasn't been drinking, has he, Slocum?"

"All he talked about coming out here was you."

"Well, I'll be damned." She took his face in both her hands and kissed the fire out of him. "Hell, yes, I'll marry you and try to behave like a wife."

"Good. Now I need to help Slocum find him."

"I bet he's been warned you two are here."

"Where does he drink at?" Slocum asked.

"The Longhorn, or the California Saloon."

"Stay here a minute," Tom said to both of them. "I'm

going to buy her a dress from one of these woman that she can wear going out of here."

She laughed. "If they have one to sell."

"Stay here. I'll be back shortly."

After Tom ran off, she looked over at Slocum and shrugged. "You know he courted me in Texas when I was just a kid. I'd never've thought he wanted me."

"He rode out with me to the ranch to help me arrest Spurlock, but I knew then he was going to use it to convince you to marry him."

"I feel like crying. An hour ago, I was ready to commit suicide over my choosing Spurlock to run off with, and here I am a giddy girl crying about Tom finding me. I'm in your debt."

"No, but you don't get many chances to start over in life, and Tom is a solid one to take you there."

"I know that. I just wouldn't have ever imagined him coming back for me."

Out of breath, Tom came in the shack, a dress over his arm. "This should fit you, Jenny Doll."

She held it open in front of herself, slung the blanket aside, slipped into the many-times-washed dress, quickly buttoned the front, and then sighed. "Thanks, Tom."

"After we collect him, I'm buying you a real dress and a train ticket for two back to North Platte, Mrs. McCall."

"I'm ready."

"Will you be my best man?" he asked Slocum.

"I can try."

"Do we wait here or go look for him?"

"I'm like her. He's cagey as a cat and may know by now that we're here."

"Should we go uptown and see if he's there?"

"Yes. Then, if he's run, we can have a wedding."

"Oh, my, you two are so fast. A wedding today?"

Slocum laughed at her. "That isn't anything. You will be on that train in no time going home."

"Well, maybe spend one night in a hotel," Tom said and hugged her.

When they asked, the bartender in the Longhorn Saloon said a ragged drunk came in an hour earlier, hit Spurlock up for some money, and for five dollars the old bearded drunk told him something the bartender couldn't hear. Whatever he told him sent Spurlock for his horse and he rode off. That was the last he'd seen of him.

Slocum nodded at Tom. "Time for you to go get married."

"She'd like a bath and a new dress."

"After you get married, you can stop, buy her a dress, and get a bath at the hotel."

"Where will you go?" Tom asked as they walked out the batwing doors.

"Jenny?" Slocum asked, with her sitting behind the cantle on Tom's saddle waiting for them. "Where did he say he was going next?"

"Billings, I think."

"Good, I know the way. Let's go and get you two hitched. I'll catch him on the way."

"Really. I wanted—"

"Slocum has a plan. Move up in the saddle to the seat. I'll ride in back," said Tom.

She managed to move forward, and he gave her the reins, then grabbed the horn and swung up in place behind her.

"Get married. Then buy you a dress and take a bath at the hotel," said Slocum.

She smiled and shook her head. "You two don't miss one damn thing."

"He don't want you backing out on him." Slocum reined his horse around.

"Oh, I bet that's right." She patted his leg beside her. "I love you, Tom McCall."

"Good thing. It's been a helluva long ride over here to find you."

She shook her head. "Folks will think we're drunk, me riding double and in a dress, and us laughing all the time."

"More fun than I've had in a long time, dear," Tom said, and Slocum nodded.

Tom saw the sign first: JUSTICE OF THE PEACE—WEDDINGS ANY TIME OF DAY.

"That must mean us," he said and jumped down at the hitch rack. Then he lifted her off the horse.

"Anyone have a hairbrush?" she asked in a desperate voice.

"I have one." Slocum dug it out of his saddlebags.

"You two stand right here. Before I marry you, Tom McCall, I'm going to brush my hair. I never imagined I'd get married like this—never even thought about it in this fashion. A worn-out dress and filthy as a sow in a muddy lot."

When she dropped her arm from the task, Tom hugged and kissed her. "It won't matter, dear. It won't matter."

Slocum put the brush back and followed them inside.

They met Judge Collins and his wife, Martha. The marriage license was done up correct and proper, the ceremony was short, and Collins signed it. Tom kissed the bride, and so did the best man.

"Take good care of him. He's a good, loyal friend and a worthwhile guy."

"I know," she whispered. "I don't know—"

Slocum silenced her with his finger on her mouth. "He knew damn good and well why he wanted you, Mrs. McCall."

"I guess he did. I will always remember you brought him to me. Thanks so much for doing that."

Slocum shook Tom's hand and wished both of them good luck, then left them. In a long jog, he headed Bull north out of Cheyenne. He slept the night in his bedroll, watered the horse at a rancher's windmill tank, then jogged on north. Tom and her would be riding the train back home for their reunion with the old man. Nice thing to happen to him.

The next day, he recalled the village where they hung the kidnapping horse thief. He turned off the road to head toward the small cluster of stores and saloons. It was early in the day, and a horse stood hipshot at the horse rack. He hitched Bull beside him. Then, after a glance to be certain no one could see him, he undid the saddlebag straps on the other horse. There was what he had expected to find in it—a woman's blue dress.

Immediately, he knew that had to be Spurlock's horse and Jenny Doll's dress. Too unusual for another man to have a dress in his saddlebags. There was a chill in the air that morning, and the sudden gust of wind drew goose bumps on the back of Slocum's arms. He tested his gun in the holster. It was loose enough to draw, if he needed to. The cylinder held five cartridges, and he knew he could use the weapon. But the one question he carried in his mental process always was, Was he fast enough?

Time would tell. He stepped up on the wooden porch. Then he came in through the winged doors of the saloon. It took a second for his eyes to adjust to the shady conditions inside, and he made out a man at the bar and a bartender. He had expected Spurlock to be taller than the cowboy standing at the bar.

"Howdy, stranger. Come on inside. What will it be?" the bartender asked.

"Who owns that horse outside?"

"That's me. I just traded for him," the man leaning on the bar said.

"How long ago?"

"Yesterday, on the road. He gave me forty dollars and took my good horse, plus gave me that one."

"Did he say where he was going?"

"Montana."

"You knew him?"

"No, but he said there were some guys tracking him. I wondered then who they were. Must have been you?"

"It was me. My partner got married in Cheyenne. I saw her dress in the saddlebags before I came in. Figured he was here."

"You're welcome to take it back to her."

Slocum shook his head. "I'll buy my new friend a beer, and me one, too. I won't be passing by where they live soon enough."

His name was Ernest, and he was going to Cheyenne in a day or so. The description of the horse he traded was simple: a bay gelding, five years old, and a Double-7 brand on his right shoulder. Slocum thanked the man, left, and rode around the back way. He looked in Mrs. Kelly's barn. There were no recently used saddles where he put Bull in the stall. Then he went and knocked on the door under her vine-covered porch.

She answered and blinked at him. "Slocum?" Then she snatched him inside by the sleeve.

"Your husband is still gone?"

She furrowed her brow. "He won't be back for six weeks. Oh, yes, thank you for stopping." Then she led him to the kitchen table. "I have hot water and some good black tea. Will you have some?"

"If you will sit on my lap while I sip it?"

"I—I will." Then, as if slightly embarrassed, she went to fix his tea.

"Are you after more criminals?" She glanced back from her preparations.

"Yes, a bank robber in Kansas who told everyone he was me."

"Oh, that's terrible."

"How have you been?"

"Busy canning the last of my garden. You know, frost will be knocking on our door soon."

"And Mr. Kelly?"

"He's hauling freight to the White River Sioux reservation. He will be months getting back home."

The teacup set before him, she raised her dress hem to sit on his lap. Then, with her looking very stiff in place, he kissed her. "Are you shaking?"

"I fear I will always shake being so close to you." She leaned her forehead to his head. "I don't want you to think I don't appreciate you dropping by, but I never expected to see you again."

"We both must be lonesome."

"A nice word."

"You're a nice friend to me."

She hugged him. "I'm addicted to you."

He turned and kissed her, then took another sip. "Should I finish my cup?"

A nod was all she gave.

He downed the rest of his tea, shifted her in his arms, and carried her off to her bedroom. Going sideways through the bedroom doorway, he gently set her on the bed. She unpinned her brown hair, and it fell in long tresses on her shoulders. Then, with her head tilted back, she gathered and tied it behind her.

She rose and began to undo his shirt buttons, swallowing

hard at her chore. He smiled, and noticing her shaky hands, he helped her. Their affair not only brought out her doubt, but also strained her mental quandary over what was right and wrong—overridden by her strong need to be taken away by a lover. Did her husband even pay her any attention when he was home? Slocum wondered. He would probably never know the minute details. She kept that sheltered in another file.

He undressed her and carefully put her dress across a chair so it didn't get wrinkled. In the dimly lit room, when he pulled the undergarment over her head, the light shone on her smooth skin, perfect breasts, and shapely butt. He undressed and swept her into his arms. They quickly became intensely connected and went off in a wild flight of pleasure that seemed to continue forever.

At last, as they lay on their backs side by side, she blew out her breath. "I am not even thinking clear. This was such an . . . overwhelming thing. Like some great monster, it swallowed and then spit me out."

"That's easy. You're a great lover."

"For you."

"Why not him?"

She shook her head and then sniffed. "It is not a pleasure for him. It is an act he must perform. No place for any savoring."

"I can't help him." He rolled over and cupped her breast. "Let's forget him and just enjoy our night together."

"Yes," she whispered and rolled over to be against him.

He left before dawn. For breakfast, he ate some cookies she gave him and put a loaf of her fresh baked bread in his saddlebags. In a short lope, he sent Bull up the road north. The sun rose, and he went on to find his man. Two days later he reached the Fort Douglas community and slept in the hay at the livery. There was frost on the grass the next morning and lots of clouds had gathered. The sky looked like the belly of a gray goose as he undid the new jacket Verna Lee had given him. With his warm coat on, he set out to ask bartenders and onlookers if they had seen Spurlock.

According to the employees, he hadn't stopped at any of the four liveries. That could mean he had a place to stay where he could also put up his horse. None of the other stables held his horse. If he had stopped there, the horse was put in a private corral or barn. Everyone had horses to ride, or drive, or work, so there were plenty of places to park one.

The bartenders Slocum spoke to didn't recall Spurlock from the reward poster he showed them. He visited a few whorehouses, but in the daytime most of the soiled doves were asleep, and those awake hadn't seen Spurlock. Slocum was thinking he was on a loose end there, when a woman stopped him on the street. She looked around as if to see if they drew any attention.

"If you are the man asking about Spurlock, I can tell you he has gone on north."

"You know him?"

"What I told you is all you need to know."

He removed his hat. "I'm plumb beholden to you."

"No need in that."

"He leave last night or this morning?"

"I told you—"

"No, did you shelter him last night?"

"Let me by you."

"Answer my question."

"I slept with him last night. There, now you know."

"Are those facilities available tonight?"

She frowned. "With you?"

He looked around. "Is there anyone else here?"

"My house is on Garrison. Number 31. Come around to the back door."

"Thanks. My name's Slocum."

"I know that. Mine is Harriet—Harriet McCoy."

"Thank you."

"Thank you, my a— You've probably already ruined my reputation in this town." She stalked away, not looking back.

He shook his head. What the hell had he done? How did she become Spurlock's overnight hostess? Why did she stop him and tell him Spurlock had left? No telling, but it sounded like he didn't need a hotel room, nor would he sleep in the hay another night. Well, he better go find a meal—she never mentioned feeding him, so he better eat before learning all about Spurlock's stopover.

The food in the café was better than he'd expected. And for thirty-five cents he had lots of fresh sliced bread, roast beef, mashed potatoes and gravy, green beans, and apple cobbler. The coffee was fresh. He walked down the street, found number 31, and walked around to the back door. Looking around and seeing nothing out of place to him, he knocked and waited.

She soon came, opened it, and smiled. "Hello." Then she let him in.

"I hope I didn't dent your reputation any more."

"Being a widow, I have to maintain my reputation."

"How do you know Spurlock?"

"Have a seat, Mr. Slocum." She showed him to the sofa, then took a seat apart from him. "He is my cousin."

"Oh, so he imposed on you."

"I would say he did. I knew he had been in much trouble. He told me he'd robbed a large bank in Abilene and used your name as his."

"Did he say I was trailing him?"

"He said he thought you'd about trapped him in Cheyenne, but he could get away from you anytime he wanted."

"Glad he's so confident."

"I found him to be a braggart and a blowhard. He spoke

of leaving a woman naked and tied up." She shook her head as if she couldn't continue saying any more.

"Jenny Doll Sawyer. He promised he'd marry her and then he treated her like a slave. We found her tied up. Tom McCall, who has known her for years, married her the next day and they went back to the ranch."

She was laughing. "He did what?"

"Married her and took her home."

"Good for him."

"I thought the same thing. Spurlock, besides tying her up, took her dress, and we had to buy her an old dress to take her into Cheyenne. So she got married in an old dress. After that, her husband took her to buy a new dress and get a bath at the hotel and their honeymoon before they caught the train to go back to Ogallala."

"Was she happy she married him?"

"Oh, yes. She was pleased. Your cousin showed her such a terrible time she was glad to marry Tom."

"My husband was killed in a stagecoach crash six months ago. I didn't know how my cousin even knew where I lived, but he came knocking yesterday, and I was shocked. Then I became disgusted with his bragging, so when I heard that you were here looking for him I had to tell you."

"Do you have a suitable single man courting you?"

"No. A few married ones have approached me. I've turned their offers down."

"You're a good housekeeper. Stand up. Turn around. You have a nice figure. How old are you?"

"Thirty. May I sit down?"

"Sure. Write down your name and address. I find men all the time that need a good woman."

She looked at him with a suspicious glare.

"Listen. You get off your high horse. If I send a man here, you need to know he's going to be serious."

"How could I—"

"Harriet. You can be a seductive lady, if you want to have a man in your life."

"I am not a dove. I can live safely for a few years on the proceeds of my husband's business."

"Harriet, with a mate, you can live in your accustomed way of life longer."

She dropped her chin. "I am too proud."

"When you stopped me today, you didn't have to do that."

"Sorry, but I'm not over losing John. I'm not ready to marry another man."

"Well, so much for that."

"I invited you here because I didn't want you to think I was a shady lady. I let him in, not for my pleasure but because he was a relative. He's the one upset me by his boasting about all the things he did wrong and him taking advantage of me, as well."

"I understand. What if I kissed you?"

"Kissed me?"

"Hell, you've been kissed before."

"I-I don't know."

He reached over, took her by the arms, drew her to him, and kissed her. When they parted, she wet her lips and spoke softly. "I don't know who you are. Lawman or another outlaw, but you can kiss me until the cows come home."

That said, she scooted over beside him. On the couch, hip to hip, they kissed some more and soon were in each other's arms. The further they went, the harder she breathed, and at last, she laid her head back on the couch and held her hand to her forehead.

"Can I do something for you?" he asked.

"While I hate to ask you, but if we are going to continue— you are going to have to unlace my corset. It's cutting off my wind."

Harriet unbuttoned her dress and shook it off, then tossed it on the other end of the couch.

"Close your eyes."

He did as she said and she pulled the slip off over her head. Then, with her on her knees, he could see the lacing of her corset. "You don't need to wear this contraption, you have a beautiful body."

She glanced back and in a little voice asked, "Do you think so?"

His fingers were working hard to pull the garment free of its binds. When it was finally stripped of the cords, he slipped his hands under the shell and weighed her breasts as he pushed it off.

She gave a soft "Oh."

"You're a real woman."

"Can we go in the bedroom?"

"Sure."

On the bed, both of them undressed now, they were soon lost in waves of passion. The fussy woman on the street melted into a creature of defined sexual desire. All those nights without any fire fanned the flames. The once icy lady became the hot fireplace feeding him the lightning bolts of pleasure that they shared until they crashed and slept.

She made him breakfast, not concerned about who saw him leave her place, and kissed him sweetly before he stepped out the door.

"When your man comes, I know what I must do."

He kissed her forehead and left her.

At the stable, he saddled Bull and rode up the road north. It was a long way to go to Billings; maybe he'd catch Spurlock before he got there. Making Bull jog-trot, he headed north.

15

The days grew colder. He slept many nights off the road so he didn't become another victim of road agents that prowled the way. His horse held up well, and at stores and from farmers he frequently bought him grain to fuel him. He finally reached Buffalo and stabled his horse. After a good sit-down meal, he spent the rest of the day canvassing stores and bars for anyone who might have seen Spurlock.

He was in a small print shop when he showed the man Spurlock's poster, and with a nod, the shopkeeper used his fingers to tap the poster. "He *vas cheer* yesterday."

"What did he want?"

"He *vanted* a blank land deed."

"Did you sell him one?"

"Oh, yah."

"What the hell did he want one for? He don't own any land here."

"Oh, der is a farm east of here he is going to buy."

"What's the name of the place?"

"The Cripes Farm. You go east two miles, turn south on that road, and go down on the creek."

"You think he's there?"

"Oh, yeah. He is courting that man's *vidow*."

Slocum still had several hours' daylight, so he rode that way. Considering Spurlock must be there, he stopped short of the place he thought was the one. His horse hobbled and out of sight, he used his brass telescope to view the place and spotted a blond woman working in a great garden. Then he saw Spurlock come out and talk to her.

Scanning him, Slocum laughed. That no-account was not doing any work. Well, anyway, at least Slocum knew he was there. Now he needed to catch him sleeping and take him prisoner. If the Buffalo sheriff would hold him until Kansas authorities could come for him, he'd have him locked him up there. If not, he'd have to take him closer, and he would.

Many county departments didn't have enough funds to pick up their prisoners. Some counted on deputy U.S. marshals to bring them back, but that depended on their funds, too. Slocum was not going to have Spurlock turned loose just because they weren't coming to get him.

Spurlock obviously had this widow woman convinced, like he'd had Jenny Doll. He must be a smooth operator. He couldn't have beat Slocum up there but by a few days, and he'd already moved in on her.

Well, his days as a con man were going to be shortened. Slocum rose to his feet, checked his six-gun, got a length of rope from his saddlebags to tie Spurlock's hands behind his back, and started toward the clapboard house. He went through the pole fencing and came across a field of corn stalks all bound up in large bundles for winter feed. He reached the back of a shed that housed a calf and a milk cow. No one was in there, so he skirted the building and made his way beside the house, ducking under a closed window and stepping up on the front porch.

They were eating supper at the table.

"Don't move." He stepped in the door with his gun in hand.

He checked Spurlock for weapons and told him to stand. He holstered his own gun and quickly tied Spurlock's hands, then forced him to sit down.

"Who . . . who are you?" the lady asked.

"He's that sumbitch robbed the bank in Kansas," Spurlock said. "He's arresting me for what he did."

"You tell that woman one more lic and I'll gag you. Mrs. Cripes, this man tied up a woman he had promised to marry. Stripped her naked and tied her up so she couldn't escape, and left her there to starve while he ran away."

She looked at Spurlock like she didn't know him. "You did that?"

"No, he's lying. He's the bank robber and killer."

"I'm taking him to the sheriff in Buffalo. You can claim his horse from there and it will be yours. He'll have no need for it where he's going. If I am lying, as he says, then the sheriff won't hold him. But, believe me, he will hold him."

She began to cry.

"Help me saddle his horse. I need to get him back to town."

She rushed out the door, moaning how she had been deceived. He jerked Spurlock up and herded him for the door. His prisoner stiffened like he wasn't going.

"I'll bust you over the head and take you belly-down on that damn horse."

"I should of killed you in Cheyenne."

"You missed your chance."

"Jails won't hold me."

"A fifty-pound ball will. I'll see they put one on you."

"If I ever—"

"Don't threaten me. When you get out of prison, you'll be too old to do anything."

Mrs. Cripes had the horse saddled, and she huddled in the corner of the shed, sobbing. Slocum stopped Spurlock and spoke to her.

"He has lied to women before and hurt them. He bought a blank deed yesterday so he could sell your farm. You were fortunate I came by before he did that."

She nodded and tossed her braids back. "I believed him. Thank you."

With Spurlock in the saddle and the horse on a lead, Slocum took him to where Bull waited. Then he rode for Buffalo. The sun was setting in the west beyond the majestic Big Horn Mountains. Bull jog-trotted, and the Double-7 branded gelding beside him made good time. They were at the county jail before darkness engulfed the town.

Slocum marched Spurlock up the steps and into the sheriff's office. A balding man looked up from behind the desk. "You a bounty man?"

"This man is Billy Hank Spurlock. He held up the Abilene, Kansas, bank last summer, and I want the five-hundred-dollar reward to go to Mrs. Cripes."

"That's damn sure unusual. Why her?"

"Because he lied to her and about swindled her out of her farm."

The deputy fished a key out of his desk. "You want to free him?"

"Not unless you chain him to the cell. He's escaped many jails."

"I can do that."

"He's lying," Spurlock said.

The deputy smiled at him. "Yeah, I bet you're a real star prisoner."

The man had Slocum fill out the prisoner papers and his own.

"Will the sheriff wire the law in Kansas and see if they will send someone to come get him? I don't want him turned loose up here."

"I can do that in the morning. The sheriff is in Cheyenne for a meeting. We won't turn him loose unless they refuse him, and then we'll give you the chance to take him."

"Good. I'll check back."

"Your name is Slocum?" He read the paper he'd filled out. "You must be tough, chasing him this far."

"Just tougher than him, is all."

The deputy, Hans Schmitt, thanked Slocum, and he went to sleep in the stables.

In the morning, someone drove up in a wagon and in a slight Germanic accent asked where Slocum was.

There in the sunlight streaming in the door, braids piled on her head, in a fresh dress, with hands on her hips, stood Mrs. Cripes. "What are you doing sleeping in the straw? Come with me. I will brush you off."

"I'm sorry," he said, using two hands to clear the stems off his clothes.

"Why did you give the reward to me?"

"How did you learn that?"

"My name is Heidi. I was a Schmitt. You took Spurlock to my brother, the deputy, last night. He sent his oldest boy early this morning to tell me what you did with the reward. The café is only a block away. I want to buy you breakfast."

"I can do that."

"No, you saved my life, my farm, and saved me from him."

"Heidi, I am so glad I saved you. He won't swindle another woman for twenty years."

"They said you wait for news from them?"

"It will be a few days, I guess."

"He can send the word to you at my house. I have a bed for you to sleep in, no hay pile."

"What about your reputation?"

She shook her head. "They can talk if they want. I can raise crops better than most men. They can whisper. I won't hear them."

Seated in the café, they ordered breakfast, and he enjoyed her company. Afterward, he hitched Bull behind her wagon, and they talked all the way to her place, about the country and farming. The next few days he helped her put the corn shocks in the shed, grateful she had hired two teenage boys to help her shock it before he got there.

It was four days of them making love at night and working crops in the daytime before Kansas officials agreed to send two deputies to Buffalo, Wyoming, and return William Hank Spurlock to Abilene, Kansas, for trial. They also sent the reward money to Heidi.

Satisfied that all had worked out, Slocum squeezed her tight and swung her around. Then he kissed her good-bye and rode off southbound on Sitting Bull. The cold air grew colder, and before he was halfway back to Cheyenne the snow came. Under the cover of snow and night, he went to Harriet's back door and knocked.

"Why, Slocum, get in here. Where did you come from?"

"Why, Harriet, I thought you'd never ask me." Snow and all, he hugged her in her robe and nightgown. Kissed her hard.

She hugged him back, and they danced around her kitchen in a polka. A fine night to be out of the snowstorm, and a good night to share with her.

"He's in jail?" She was out of breath when they quit.

"He's going to be in a Kansas jail. They're hauling him back."

"Oh, I thought you were sending me a man."

"I'll have to substitute for him tonight."

"Good, I'll like you better, I bet, than him."

"No, when I find him, he will be a real man."

A month later, Slocum sat on the patio looking across at the shabby remains of the historical Alamo. Two young ladies entertained, clacking castanets and dancing for him and the gentleman in the chair beside him.

The man asked, "This lady you speak about is in Wyoming?"

"Josh, she's thirty years old, a widow woman, and a good housekeeper. You write her, then send her the money to come down and examine your situation. Offer her the money to go back if she doesn't like it or you. Harriet is a sweet woman, who originally came from Texas. She has a nice figure, dresses well, and is educated."

"I'll be forty in six months."

"I don't think that'll bother her. You lead an active life and entertain people. Your house is a castle."

"She didn't poison her dead husband?"

Slocum laughed and shook his head.

"No children?"

"No kids."

"I'll write her."

He handed him Harriet's name and address on a piece of paper. "You'll be proud."

"Good. I better go write a letter and post it."

Slocum laughed and shook his head. He'd promised Harriet he'd find her a good man.

Mail proved slow between the two, but before Slocum left San Antonio in the spring, she got on a stage, train, and more trains and arrived in town.

His friend, Josh, came by his table on the square the third day. "She's exactly what you promised. I plan to marry her in two weeks. Will you be here for the wedding?"

"No. I need to go see a friend who's having a range war and thinks I can settle it for him."

"I must go to Houston for a few days to close some business. I am so glad you knew her and pointed me toward her. She's a born Texan and certainly a nice lady."

"I never tell you lies, do I?"

"No, but a man can't be too careful picking a wife."

"Have a safe trip and tell her I wish you both good fortune."

That evening, someone knocked on Slocum's door.

He drew his Colt and answered it. It was Harriet.

"Well, let me in," she hissed, and he did.

She threw down her shawl. "Josh said you had to leave town. I was afraid the servants might talk, so I came out here before you left. He's gone to Houston. I wanted one more night with you."

"Have the two of you made love?"

She looked shocked at him. "Why, no, we aren't married yet."

"Oh."

She turned her back to him. "Get me out of this corset, please. I can't breathe."

"Silly thing. Why do you wear it?"

"To seduce you."

He laughed out loud.

She shed the top of her dress and he fumbled at the strings in back. "It works every time. Harriet, you are a devil."

"You know I won't do this again with you after I marry him."

"Really?"

She turned her head and frowned at him. "I think so. There you have it— Oh, your hands feel so good."

He smiled. Now, if he only knew about his Cheyenne princess. He hoped she'd found someone, too. A pleasant evening ahead for him with Josh's wife-to-be, but he wondered if the snow was off the road going north.

His friend, Abe Summers, needed some help on this range war business. He better go check that out. He breathed in her heavenly perfume. Tonight, he'd savor her body like no other—in the morning, he'd be headed north on a stage to Fort Worth.

Watch for

SLOCUM AND THE PACK OF LIES

427th novel in the exciting SLOCUM series
from Jove

Coming in September!

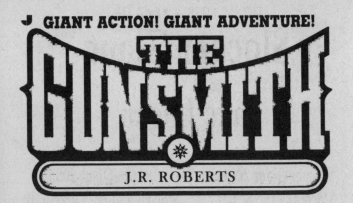

GIANT ACTION! GIANT ADVENTURE!

THE GUNSMITH

J.R. ROBERTS

penguin.com/actionwesterns

M455AS0812

GIANT-SIZED ADVENTURE FROM AVENGING ANGEL LONGARM.

BY TABOR EVANS

penguin.com/actionwesterns

M456AS0812

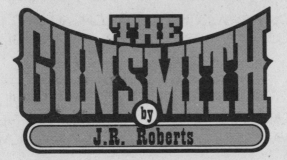